P9-CQJ-514

Winter Run

ALSO BY ROBERT ASHCOM

*Lost Hound: And Other Hunting Stories
and Poems*

Winter Run

by

ROBERT ASHCOM

A Shannon Ravenel Book

ALGONQUIN BOOKS
OF CHAPEL HILL
2002

ℝ

A SHANNON RAVENEL BOOK
Published by
ALGONQUIN BOOKS OF CHAPEL HILL
Post Office Box 2225
Chapel Hill, North Carolina 27515-2225

a division of
Workman Publishing
708 Broadway
New York, New York 10003

JAN   9 2003

"Winter Run" originally appeared in a slightly different
version in *Oasis: A Literary Magazine,* to whose editors
grateful acknowledgment is made.

This is a work of fiction. While, as in all fiction, the literary
perceptions and insights are based on experience, all names,
characters, places, and incidents are either products of the
author's imagination or are used fictitiously. No reference to
any real person is intended or should be inferred.

Library of Congress Cataloging-in-Publication Data
Ashcom, Robert L.
      Winter run / by Robert Ashcom.
         p. cm.
      "A Shannon Ravenel book."
      ISBN 1-56512-328-X
      1. Boys—Fiction.   2. African American agricultural
laborers—Fiction.   3. Human-animal relationships—
Fiction.   4. Male friendship—Fiction.   5. Race
relations—Fiction.   6. Hunting dogs—Fiction.
7. Farm life—Fiction.   8. Virginia—Fiction.   I. Title.
PS3551.S366 W46 2002
813'.54—dc21   2002023204

10 9 8 7 6 5 4 3 2 1
First Edition

THIS BOOK IS OFFERED TO THE

GLORY OF GOD

AND IN LOVING MEMORY OF

MARY LEWIS ASHCOM

A C K N O W L E D G M E N T S

I would like to thank William Woodward for his
serendipitous help; Jacques de Spoelberch, my agent,
for getting me going; and Shannon Ravenel, my editor,
for her insight and patience.

CONTENTS

Winter Run

Gretchen's Arms

IT WAS A DARK DAY. Water glistened black on the sidewalks. The naked branches of the trees lining the street hung overhead like webbed fingers on crooked arms. Another two degrees and it would all be frozen. Everything was close, everything held tight, bare hands clenched in pockets.

There were new buildings and a lot of construction around the hospital. But I couldn't mistake the smell once I walked through the doors. The color-coded lines on the walls were supposed to guide me to my destination. They didn't make any sense. Finally a nurse gave up explaining and just took me to the ward.

And there she was. I would hardly have recognized her. The disease had taken her away. Who would have ever thought that so much flesh was necessary to make a face. Hers was gone. Skin stretched taut over the bones that everyone said were the source of her beauty. Bones. People had talked about them. She was unmistakably Scandinavian. In youth her creamy white blond hair had fallen to her shoulders. She wore it that way even after it turned silver. She had been tall, willowy, with slender arms. Arms always waiting for me, reaching out to take me back. But not now. It was too late. This time I was sure. Her rings were gone. They had looked foreign on her long, tapered fingers, anyway.

I watched her. Her cool slate-gray eyes were closed, her breath rising and falling, the kind of breathing you do when you are in pain. Tubes. The whole nine yards.

All my life I called her Gretchen except in loaded moments. Then she became Mother—the Swedish orphan, raised by friends after her parents both died of cancer within a single year. The friends were Catholic and strict. Gretchen was expected to understand the doctrine of the Trinity. But she never had. How could one thing be three? Or the other way around? She was defiant. And so for the rest of her life she received the sacrament in her left hand although she was right-handed.

"Hello Mother." Her body shifted slightly.

Then the idiot question: "How are you?"

"Fine."

What do you say to the already as-good-as-dead—to one whose rings and bracelets have been removed? I put my hand on her wrist. It was cold and very small.

"I am here. Is there anything I can do for you?"

"No thank you." In clear English.

There followed two days of tension and suspense, arguments with doctors about pain medication, about the chances of her coming back. I knew she wouldn't, not looking like that. She knew how she looked.

I had to leave for a few days. I told her what I was doing. She came up from wherever it was she was and said, "Before you go, make a list of your choices and put it on the chair. I never approved of them—but put it on the chair." Then she went away again.

My choices? My choices? What do you mean?

I couldn't breathe. It was like suffocation from the dust around a grain bag when it is being filled. The dust is like ether and the world spins. And your eyes swim. You raise your head and the far wall of the feed mill looks obscured as if by rain. That was what it was like—sitting on a steel chair in that room, with my choices.

And then the world lit up the way it did once as I was leading a stallion out to his paddock on a spring Sunday morning. It happened just as I opened the gate to let him through. And for a moment everything was revealed to me. Then it was gone.

It happened again there in that hospital room. This time the revelation was a story.

VIRGINIA IN THE LATE FORTIES. The end of summer—days echoing with the bobwhite's call and the incessant cooing of the mourning doves. The honeysuckle had lost its scent, and on the real farms the corn was tasseled and high, about ready to gather. Blackberries were in, though I didn't have the patience for them. But Gretchen made preserves, so sometimes I had to pick them. They were worse than shelling walnuts. It was the brink of fall. Soon the air would be full of wood smoke, and it would be hunting season.

The farm was huge—almost seven hundred acres. But there were no crops, just pastures mostly gone to broom sage and a couple of garden plots and the little pasture where the milk cow lived by herself except when Bat, the mule, was living at Silver Hill.

There was also the four-acre fenced lot where the hogs were kept. There were huge oaks in the enclosure, and in the fall the hogs could live off the acorns. The rest of the time Matthew fed them the leftovers from the house and commercial feed from the co-op. The hog lot was completely surrounded by the broom sage field above the pond. The hog lot was like a fortress in the middle of the field. It had been tightly fenced and refenced over the years. The fence was thick with honeysuckle and multiflora rose. Deep in the middle was a spring coming out from under a rock. The spring flowed its muddy trickle to the fence and then down the hill to the pond, carrying the hog waste. We didn't know any better in those days. Even in a drought, the place was always muddy. It had become a sinkhole.

Paradise trees and cedars had grown up to the

point where you couldn't see into the place except where the hunt club had put in chicken coop jumps— those paneled A-frames that straddled the wire fence, allowing the huntsmen and horses a safe jump into the hog lot if that's where the fox and hounds led them. It took a special horse to jump into that place, with the mud and slop. Horses hate hogs. So what usually happened was the riders stood next to the fence, listening as the hounds gave tongue in the frantic way they have when they are close. Add to that the oinking and squealing of the hogs and the horses hating the smell and refusing to stand still, and it was mayhem. But thrilling.

That August, on the first day of foxhunting—called cubbing—the hounds were brought to the farm to hunt. I had a pony and would ride with the hunt later that year, but on this day Matthew and I stood above the lot and watched the whole thing from the burnt-out summerhouse yard. Sure enough the fox had run into the hog lot, with the hounds in hot pursuit. I kept looking up at Matthew saying, "They'll kill him! They'll kill him!" Feeling awful for the fox but cheering for the hounds in my mind at the same time.

"Be patient, Charlie," he said. "Quit your jumping up and down and watch. Be still, Charlie. Be still!"

Around and around the hounds went, now coming to our side, then straight toward the jump on the other side. I was sure the fox would come out and take off in the open. Crescendo after crescendo. The hogs were squealing and running—apparently with the hounds, the whole huge group in pursuit of the fox. It was outrageous and wild, as if something from time beyond memory had been turned loose, broken loose from whatever shackles time could have contrived for it—the sound and the hounds—and our wild imaginations. I could feel the tension in Matthew next to me, too. What was really happening? After twenty minutes of unbearable suspense, the huntsman decided to go in on foot and round up the hounds, and to hell with this mess. So in he went, blowing the horn and hollering for the hounds. The whips stood around the enclosure cracking their whips and hollering, "Get to him!" at the top of their lungs. I wanted to go in, too, but of course Matthew wouldn't let me. Finally the huntsman emerged, covered from head to foot in mud and hog slop. The hounds were behind him. They were also covered. They were panting and shaking their heads and tails and looking thoroughly satisfied, in contrast to the huntsman who was thoroughly furious and told everyone so, including the Master.

I pulled on Matthew's arm, "They killed him, didn't they? They killed that fox in there? Why did the huntsman let them go in there?"

"Charlie, be still," he said again. "Be still and watch!"

So for twenty minutes we squatted next to the huge poplar and watched. The last hound had come out, covered in mud and glory, the whips hollered, "Pack up!" and the hunt left to find another fox. Still we watched. Then Matthew pointed to a patch of honeysuckle, as a darkening shadow emerged. I held my breath and gripped his sleeve. The fox stopped as he came into the open. Looked around.

He was covered in mud also. He looked like a half-drowned cat. He shook himself, and as his coat dried, he became twice as big. Then he trotted off, his ears pulled back to hear if anything happened behind him.

"Now Charlie, if we wouldn't of been down wind of him, that fox would of smelled us and never come out until we were gone. Do you see, Charlie? Do you see?" He always questioned me. Did I see?

Yes, I saw. Because the breeze was in our faces, we could have smelled the fox, had we been able, but he couldn't smell us. Yes, I saw.

I *had* to get into that place and see how with all that hell going on, with the hounds roaring around, the hogs squealing and running, and mud and slop everywhere, that fox had got out of there in one piece. How? I would find out.

For a moment the reverie ended. Is that what it had been all those years ago—the fox and the mud? Or was it the darkness and mayhem and the sounds . . . the darkness?

"Charlie, are you listening?" Then his hand was on my shoulder, and he pulled me around so he could look straight at me. "Charlie, quit! I know what you're thinking. You know that old boar hog is in there and would eat you alive."

"But—"

"But nothing. No!"

THE BIG BRICK-AND-CLAPBOARD house at the top of the hill was 175 years old and home to only Professor James and his wife. They had no children. A middle-aged black couple, Matthew Tanner and Sally, his wife, looked after the Jameses. Matthew milked the cow and took care of the gardens and, increasingly, drove the old professor where he needed to go. Matthew was a hunter and the Jameses loved wild game. In the fall each year Matthew killed a buck, even in the days when they were really scarce. He also killed a tom turkey each spring. Sometimes he was the only one in the community to accomplish this feat, the turkeys were so few and shy. He knew the woods and fields. He fit into the land and its moods and seasons like black hands into the brown cloth work gloves we all wore.

I turned nine that summer and I knew all this about him. Had known it since I was a little boy and held his coat sleeve when things got exciting or I was frightened. It wasn't thinking that told me. I just knew. We were a pair—the stout black man and the skinny, very blond white kid. Matthew and Sally had no children. Maybe that was it.

Later in the week of the cubbing, I walked up the hill to the big house to find Matthew. As I crossed the front porch I heard the professor talking and chuckling in his wheezy voice. "I know, Matthew. I should never have bought those five old sows from the Gibsons. But Ronnie has been sick and things are hard for them right now. Just try. And maybe that old boar will get them bred. If not, we'll slaughter the barren ones. Although God knows what we'll do with the meat. Those old things must be as tough as a rubber tire. You'll just have to feed them feed from the co-op. We sure don't have enough leftovers with just you and Sally and Mrs. James and me." There was a pause. "Oh, and Matthew—don't let Charlie Lewis near that boar!"

I knocked on the door and pulled it open.

"Ah, and there you are, Charlie," said the professor. "Did you hear what I said? Do not go near that boar without Matthew. Is that clear? I heard about the hunt you witnessed and your interest in that place."

"Yes sir," I said, "but—"

"No damn buts, young man," he exclaimed. "That animal is dangerous. You mind Matthew or I'm going to talk to your mama and papa."

He was serious, and as I didn't want to be kept at home when things were happening on the farm I shut up. It was my way—push them about as far as they would go and sometimes beyond, like the time I took George Maupin's workhorse, Jim, and rode five miles up the back road bareback to ask George if I could keep the horse for the weekend before they caught me. Shortly after that they had got me the pony.

Two days later, Robert Paine, who was small and skinny and deep, deep black and had done time on the road gang, came to help Matthew move the old sows. As he always did, Robert looked sideways at me when he realized I was along for the ride. But I didn't pay it any attention and Matthew acted like he didn't see it. It would be years before the meaning of those looks became clear, before I knew the depth of his enmity, before, on a January night sitting around the fire next to the store at hog-killing time, my Eden would end.

Once the men got the old '32 Ford stake body running, we drove up the valley road to the Gibson's and loaded the sows up the pen's ramp into the truck. They protested mightily, but the men knew hogs and squeezed them into the truck without any trouble.

At the other end, Matthew backed the truck up to the gap in the hog-lot fence with its vine-covered gate barely visible. He lowered the tailgate on the truck, and the sows slid and snuffled their way down to the ground and wandered off into the jungle of vines and stumps and mud.

That evening, we went back to be sure the sows hadn't gone crazy and jumped the chicken coops. We sat on one of the jumps with our legs hanging inward. The trees in the lot had been thinned a few years back leaving four-foot-high stumps. The stumps had grown up in honeysuckle and blackberries. Each stump had a clump of dirt and grass around its base, like a little island in a sea of thick red mud and greasy puddles of brown water. It looked like a spooky Halloween garden. An evening mist was coming in, but we could see the shapes of the hogs, lying in the mud between the puddles. They looked like the larvae you find under an old board in a barn lot: pale to white and, in the mist, without real shape. Like slugs. You always hear that

pigs are intelligent, but it's hard to believe that anything that mud-caked and smelly could be intelligent.
They are, though. And they all have different person-
alities, and special eyes.

We heard one grunting a ways off and then the
huge gray boar came into sight—iron gray, with wiry
hair all over his back, swinging his head from side to
side as he walked among the prone shapes, occasionally pushing one with his nose, checking to see if she
was in heat.

The boar moved steadily in our direction.

"Hey, old hog!" Matthew called. "Are they all right,
or are they too old?" Then he turned to me. "Too old,
I reckon. But the man wants them bred. So that's
what's going to happen."

When Matthew called, the big boar had raised his
head. His eyes looked right at us, not like cows and
horses, which hardly ever will look you in the face.
His eyes were bright. They seemed to have their own
light, like the hog had a flashlight in his brain turned
on us to see what we were thinking. Does a hog oink
only through his nose? That big male rumbled, way
down in his chest. He sounded wild. I stared at him,
thinking, *What would you do if I came in there? I could
walk around checking the sows with you. And we could
look into every corner of the lot, to see if we could
find a snake. And if we did, you would eat it, because
Matthew told me a hog would eat a snake, alive—
even a copperhead—and it wouldn't hurt him.*

I know what I could do. I could bring the pony and

jump the chicken coop and ride around with you. That way I wouldn't get all muddy and make Gretchen angry. And if you really didn't like me in there, I could turn the pony around and race to the fence and jump the jump. And no harm done. And I would find out. Find out how the fox was able to run in there and come out alive. And maybe see another fox hunting for mice . . .

Looking back, it is no wonder they were all so angry with me and frightened. It was as if I somehow wanted to run back up the pipe of evolution and burst through at the other end into a meadow where nature and its creatures and I were the same thing.

"Matthew," I asked, "is that hog tame or wild? I mean, he stands there looking at us and doesn't run away, so he's not like a deer or a fox. What would he do if I went in there with him? Would he be like a cow and maybe stand still or maybe walk away—"

"Charlie!" he interrupted. "Now you listen to me. I told you before about hogs."

"Oh, I know. You mean about maybe eating you if you fell into a little pen with them. But that boar is in the open—it would be like—"

"No, it wouldn't be like anything you ever seen! That boar (he called it a "bo") is dangerous. You'll end up just like Billy Gibbons over to Smith's. They have a big pen, too. But that didn't keep them hogs from near eating him that morning he come in drunk and slipped and fell into the pen when he was calling them. Hadn't of been for the horse trainer come to check a sick yearling, and hearing all the commotion from the hog pen, Billy would of been dead! You know they had him down in the slop and had tore his clothes off, and you could see blood all over his chest where they started to eat him. They had a time getting him out of there. What with those hogs not wanting to let go of that boy and Jimmy running around yelling for help and that old woman, Mrs. Greeves, standing there laughing and saying how that would teach him to come in drunk, before she knowed how bad it was. Hadn't of been for the horse trainer, that boy would sure Lord have been dead.

"Now Charlie, I know you. And if I see you coming near this hog lot without me, I'm going to call your mama and get her to keep you home. And you know she will if I tell her. Are you listening, Charlie?"

GRETCHEN? SHE WAS ALWAYS there in the background, looking at me. At the time I understood she was afraid, but I never knew of what.

That evening she was in her garden. She was kneeling on a feed sack with a narrow trowel in her gloved right hand transplanting tulip bulbs that Mrs. James had given her. Her thick hair was pulled back with a rubber band, and there was a thin line of perspiration on her upper lip. She looked up and smiled. Her gray eyes were cool and appraising, thinking, *What have you done today, Charlie? What new, crazy thing have you gotten into today?* Not out loud, but I knew what she was thinking. Out loud she said, "Did you and

Matthew and Robert get the pigs moved?" She called them pigs. She was a city girl.

"Yes, and we saw the boar hog. He's huge, Gretchen. Huge! And he rumbles down in his chest when he moves around. He looks like a wild animal—"

Her eyes tensed. "You know you're not to go there alone. Professor James spoke to me about it. And I will speak to your father about it this weekend. You must not go near that pig lot without Matthew. Do you hear me, Charlie?"

THE PONY WAS TOUGH. The day I got her she kicked me in the right knee as I was walking into her stall to feed her. Her name was Tricksey, which I hated. To me she was just the pony. Her coat was gray, but depending on how wet the red clay of our fields was, she was pink or reddish brown. When I went to catch her in the big open broom sage pasture, she blended with the land so I could hardly see her. Sometimes I absolutely couldn't see her. She was a part of the countryside. She fit in.

She was hard to catch. Like the other things about the land and the animals I couldn't understand, I didn't understand her. But she would come to a handful of grain if I stroked my palm and wiggled the grain around in my hand.

That afternoon she was harder than usual to find. She seemed to blend into the ground even more. Maybe it was a sign. The plan was the same as the daydream: The pony and I would jump over one of the chicken coops into the hog lot. Then I would find the boar and just hang around with him.

Gretchen had gone to town, and Matthew was nowhere to be seen. We trotted down the dirt lane to the hog lot. The weather was threatening, ominous to the west over the mountains. We had passed the hog lot many times, so I was sure the pony was completely used to the smell. At the first chicken coop jump, I stopped her and looked over into the pen. No hogs in sight.

She refused twice. By the third time, I was really furious and beat her hard behind the saddle with the crop. She landed in a mud puddle and stopped dead still. And I almost fell over her head. But there I was —in the pen. From the inside, it was like a trap, with the paradise trees growing everywhere and the mud. Even the honeysuckle looked stronger. I had landed twenty feet from the rock with the little spring flowing out from under it. It bubbled up clear but quickly muddied as it started its journey to the outside world. Swamp lilies grew around the rock. It was a little garden in the sea of mud. We moved in deep enough that I couldn't see the fence behind me—or in front. It was like being out of sight of land in a boat. I had never felt the pony so alive and aware. She walked stiff-legged, with her neck rigid and her nostrils flared, looking. I loved it.

We found the sows in a group, lying on their sides in the mud with their heads up, looking startled at us with those flashlight eyes. When she saw them, the pony slammed on the brakes, again, and whirled around, right out from under me, leaving me sitting in the mud. And then she was gone, galloping back toward the chicken coop jump, whinnying in a panic. She had never been in with hogs before, not right in the pen with them. Neither, of course, had I. I got up. I looked at the sows. Not one moved. *Well*, I thought hopefully, wishing it to be so, *this will probably be fine. The sows aren't upset.*

I was standing in six inches of mud. I looked around. Through the vines, I could just see the chicken coop jump on the other side of the pen. It felt like I was way down inside something. The cloudy sky was far above. The air was close—August close.

He came from behind me. I heard the sound but didn't immediately put it together with the boar. When he rumbled in his chest, I turned around. So there I was. It was as if I had known somehow that I would be in there on the ground with that six-hundred-pound hog, figuring out what to do next. The big old sows were sprawled out in the mud in front of me with their heads still up like fat women on a beach watching as the shark's fin bears down on the swimmer.

I went for the nearest stump—which meant sloshing across five feet of mud and water. I grabbed the four-foot-high stump and frantically started to climb it. I was very frightened but also very excited. I wasn't going to let that boar get me!

The stump was rotten; it broke off at the base as

soon as I started to climb. I fell to the opposite side of its base from the hog. I got up and reached for the next one. It held and I pulled myself up using the honeysuckle vines. I must have looked like a fence lizard peering over the top of a half-round post. I figured I was about in the middle of the enclosure. The sows were still mildly interested. The boar was more interested, very interested. But all was not lost. I could see the opening of the far chicken coop through the vines, about fifty feet away. In a way it was comical. The damn thing was just a big, bristly, gray pig, looking up at me with flopped over ears, snuffling loudly through his nose. Just a pig.

But he had those flashlight eyes, and I knew the story about Billy Gibbons at the Greeveses was true. When after ten minutes the boar was still looking at me, I began to worry. Clinging to the stump was getting old. It was a sure thing I was not going to be able to wander around the hog lot checking the sows with him. There were a number of possibilities in the long run, none of them attractive. At some point someone would see the pony around the barnyard with the stirrups and reins flapping. No matter who saw the pony first, word would get to Matthew, and he would put it together and come after me and no doubt would have to shoot the hog to get me out of there—with results nearly as awful as being eaten by him. There would be no talk at the store in the evenings about how Charlie Lewis had escaped the huge-ass gray boar that had him up a stump or about how Charlie walked home, muddy but safe, to catch the pony and put her away and walk to the house to take his licks.

So I had to figure something out. The solution was not immediately apparent until the boar stopped looking at me, turned his head to eye the sows, and oinked his way over to them; then the situation started to look a little brighter. The chicken coop jump was there, a faint glimmer, a window, a way out, with about fifty feet of mud and water and roots to trip me up. Then I heard our car horn. Not just a toot. Steady. Gretchen had found the pony and was on the way up to the big house, looking for Matthew. If I was going to do it, I'd better do it quick . . .

When I finally let go of the honeysuckle to slide down the stump, the boar turned his head and forgot the sows. The the sows saw me, too, and oinked onto their feet and came with the boar, the whole damn pack of them. We were off through the mud and goo and water. I grabbed a branch and began to pole vault myself toward the chicken coop jump. The boar rumbled along behind me. He was excited. The pitch of the rumbling went up—the predator in a sight chase with his prey. I was still very frightened, but I would beat them!

It was dark in that hog lot. The paradise trees were low down with their smell like lead, and the oaks made a high canopy. The hog stink was deep in my nose. All around were the stumps sticking up above the mud and water on their mounds of dirt, like islands. But they were not for me.

I heard Matthew's truck, so she must have found him pretty quickly. They were coming for me and I didn't want to be found. I wanted to be like the fox, deep in the enclosure, fooling everyone. I could wait for Gretchen and Matthew to leave and then escape on my own. I didn't want them to be waiting for me. I wanted to do it alone.

But the boar and the sows were too close. And there was the chicken coop beckoning. I could see the daylight shining through the opening and then the truck stopping. By this time I had started yelling at myself to hurry up, because here they came! The boar was snuffling at my legs. Matthew was waving his arms. Gretchen was screaming. And then I grabbed the top board of the chicken coop and pulled myself over while the boar slammed into the wooden jump with the sows right behind him.

I landed in her arms and lay still. She wiped the mud and water from my face, smoothed back my hair, which was the same color and texture as hers, whispering, "Charlie, why do you do these things? Why don't you let the world alone?"

I knew what she meant, but she was talking about her world, not mine. She hovered over my life like a gentle bird with huge wings to clutch me to her. She held me with her strength, saying in her soul, *Come back. Let it alone. Be safe.* But I wasn't little, and I wasn't coming—not in the way she meant. Even then, and never again.

I looked up into Matthew's eyes, with their bloodshot

whites and deep brown pupils. He was angry because he was afraid. But I had needed to know. I said to him, "You see! It was just like with the hounds and that fox. Those hogs couldn't catch me. I made it through. I knew I could."

I hadn't known. But even at nine, I had had to go in there, into that dark, forbidden place.

Then in his soft voice, Matthew said, "Come on, Charlie. Let's go home." He picked me up with his huge hands as if I weighed nothing and set me firmly on my feet. "Let's go home."

Sight

BY THE AGE OF EIGHT, Charlie was crazy about horses. Maybe it was even earlier, but during that summer it came to a crisis, as things often did with Charlie and his enthusiasms. The problem began with Bat, the old one-eyed mule who was owned by Leonard Waits but seemed to spend most of her time at Silver Hill. Bat and Charlie were close, if such a thing could be said about a pale blond boy and a brown mare mule. But the fact was that they spent a lot of time with each other. The mule often jumped out of whatever pasture she happened to be in to end up where Charlie was. She even met the school bus— or at least she was usually there when the bus arrived. Many folks refused to accept the idea that a twenty-five-year-old mule would actually wait at the bus stop for a seven-year-old boy, and the fact that it often happened was written off as coincidence. Charlie talked to her just the way he would a human, and while he was on his own two feet she did almost anything he wanted. Most of the time she even followed him around loose, without a lead line, more or less like a dog.

But the relationship did not extend to riding.

The first problem was that she had a high, straight backbone that was so uncomfortable that even with a pillow Charlie could hardly bear to sit on her. The next problem was that when he was on her back, he had virtually no control over her. The way the friendship seemed to work was that when Charlie was on the ground and she could see him out of her one eye, their special relationship held. But when he was on her back and she couldn't see him—because of the blinkers on the old work bridle—he became just another human being. Most of the time she wouldn't even move. Mule nature took over. This theory was offered up by Jimmy Price who was considered an expert on horses because he had a mare named Princess who would lie down and roll over on command. Lacking any better authority, his theory was accepted. And so Bat fell from grace as transportation and, more important, as the embodiment of the romance of riding.

THE SUMMER CHARLIE was to turn eight, the woods on the far side of the farm next to the railroad were to be logged. No one was sure why. Professor

James surely didn't need the money. There had to be something, some reason, but nobody knew what it was, not even Matthew.

A white man named George Maupin, who lived ten miles west at the foot of Burdens Mountain, had the contract in the beginning. George was only five foot six, but he was absolutely square and the physical power implied in his shape was true. He always wore a businessman's hat, summer and winter. He had sweated right through it for so many years that the band was two shades darker than the rest of the hat. George was an old-fashioned logger. That meant that he had two strong workhorses, a beat-up six-ton truck with a log rack, a huge two-man chain saw with a four-foot cutting bar, his own strength, and the need for one other strong man.

Before the war came, George had been doing fine. Landowners hired him to go into old woods, take out the biggest trees for saw logs, leave the rest, and not make a mess. In those days George had four horses and could move really large logs. It was a time before we got used to the woods being torn up by skidders and bulldozers.

George's branch of the Maupin family was native to the area around the village. There were three brothers, but the home farm next to the village was not big enough for one family, let alone three, so George, just before the war, had bought a little place in Burdens Hollow at the foot of the mountain. It was not really a farm, just a rocky fifteen-acre pasture with a log house and barn, with the beginning of Burdens River running through the pasture. It was a mountain farm—there were black snails in the stream, the kind found only in mountain creeks and rivers.

When George got home from the war, he wanted to pick up where he'd left off. But now there was competition from the machines. And time was becoming money. Even so, there were still some people like the professor who cared about the woods—not many, but enough to keep George busy, at least for a while.

Because Silver Hill was so far from George's home, his two workhorses would be fed ear corn in the barn at the Corn House, where Charlie and his parents lived, and turned out in the broom sage field behind it at night. Charlie was intensely interested, as he was with anything new. Other than his unsatisfactory experience with Bat, he knew next to nothing about riding beyond the fact that you pulled on a single rein to turn left or right, both reins to stop, and kicked with your heels to go. Leonard Waits, who owned two big workhorse mares in addition to Bat, had let Charlie sit up on one of the mares a few times. Charlie had also watched Leonard put on the stiff, old work bridles with their twisted wire bits and blinkers. So he knew how to do that much. There were no saddles at the farm; the professor had long ago given up riding. Anyway, the time of horses was ending.

But not for Charlie.

• • •

MONDAY OF THE FIRST week in June, the horses had arrived in George's neighbor's cattle truck. Their heads hung so far out over the side of the truck you would have thought they would either fall out or jump out at the first intersection. But they were quiet creatures and it took a lot to surprise or scare them. The neighbor backed the truck up to a bank and off they came. To Charlie's delight.

"What's his name, Mr. Maupin? He sure is big. How old is he?" Charlie began his usual flood of questions. George Maupin knew who Charlie was, as everyone did, but he had never been around him to any extent and was surprised and amused at the rush of questions.

"His name's Jim, Charlie. I reckon he's about ten. I got him when he was a colt. Give a hundred dollars for him. I knowed the mare he come from and she was a big, strong, gentle mare. I never did hear who his daddy was. Anyway, he growed up to be a good one. Strong like his mama. And you can drop the lines on him in the woods and he won't move a step till you come back.

"Can I ride him, Mr. Maupin?"

"Well, Charlie, I don't know about that. Maybe . . ." His voice drifted off. He was a man who seldom spoke without cause, and he was a little bit amazed by Charlie. George wasn't used to little kids who talked a mile a minute in grown-up language, so he inadvertently opened the door to what was to become another one of Charlie's passions, because "maybe" always sounded like "yes" to Charlie.

Jim, who stood at least three feet taller than Charlie at the shoulder, was totally gentle. That first evening he munched his ears of corn and then stood quietly while Charlie figured out how to get the bridle on him. This problem was solved by leading the huge horse up to a fifty-five-gallon drum, after putting a hay bale next to it. Charlie then crawled up the bale onto the barrel and finally got on a level with Jim's head. Once the bridle was on, he coaxed him forward so he could leap to his back, clutching the little pillow he used for a saddle. That first evening when Matthew saw Charlie emerge from the barn, ducking his head down by the horse's withers so he wouldn't get knocked off by the overhead and clutching his pillow, he burst out laughing. Once in the barnyard Charlie put the pillow behind himself and hopped backward onto it. So there he was: the nearly eight-year-old boy, smiling in his blond way, proud that he had managed to get himself tacked up and mounted even if his charger was a gaunt and tired workhorse.

"Charlie, you can't just go riding that horse," Matthew said. "You know he don't belong to us. And, anyway, once George starts logging, this horse'll be tired from a day's work, so why should he have to put up with your foolishness after his dinner. It's his time to rest." This made sense to Charlie, but the urge to ride was stronger than his good sense.

The morning the logging began, Charlie walked

over the hill with George, who drove the team in front of him with the two rope lines and his voice. Bill, the second and much smaller and younger horse, was on the right because he still didn't completely know the commands. With Bill on the right, it was easier for Jim to pull him over when George said, "haw," the word for left, or push him when George said "gee," for right.

Richie Settle, an eighteen-year-old white boy who helped George, drove the truck in front. Richie was what we called slow. But if you spoke quietly and clearly, he could do most anything you wanted, even drive the truck across fields rather than on the public roads. He was very strong. The two-man chain saw was nothing to him. He even understood how to service it and to tighten the chain.

But Richie couldn't handle the team. The movements of the huge animals were just too much for him. He looked George in the face when George was giving him instructions, but he never looked carefully at the horses, so he never learned to anticipate what they were going to do. The truck was okay, the living animals were not. So Richie drove the truck and George drove the team, with Charlie walking along beside, pleased as he could be that something brand new was about to happen.

The process was simple. The owner of a woods to be logged called the extension agent who sent the cruiser to mark the trees to be harvested and fix the value. Then the owner contracted with a logger to come in and do the job. Just the largest logs were taken and the branches were pulled into the open and burned. Done right, there was hardly any mess left at all. Within a year the drag tracks of the logs were gone.

That was George's arrangement. There was a deadline. The professor had to have the work completed by the middle of August so he could be paid by the pulp-and-paper company by September 1. When the deal was made, the time limit seemed fine to George. But at the end of that first day, when he stopped in at the store, he sounded nervous. He said there were a lot more trees marked than he had expected. Also, some of them were so big he wasn't sure his team could skid them out. It had been a long time since he had been in those woods—at least a couple of years before the war. They had changed. He should have known.

Everyone wondered what Professor James's hurry was.

But as the team and George and Charlie and Richie had made their way across the broom sage field that first morning, time hadn't been a factor. It was a pure June morning in Virginia. The humidity had not arrived, all the spring plants and trees were in bloom, and the bobwhite had begun their insistent shout that challenged even the snarl of the chain saw. Or so we thought.

The first tree was cut. George was on the engine end of the saw, and Richie, who was on the other end, smiled in pleasure when he felt the tree start to go. As the gap opened, the men stepped back from the tree. It scythed through the surrounding branches and hit the ground with a thud that caused the earth to shake under Charlie as he stood on the edge of the woods with the team. The horses were only mildly interested, but Charlie's eyes were round and startled. He had seen small trees cut for firewood but never anything like this huge oak, which, after it crashed to the ground, looked dead, really dead.

After the large limbs were cut off with the saw, George and Richie paused to sharpen the axes they would use to strip the rest of the trunk. George sat on the tree with his legs crossed, chewing his tobacco while he moved the file slowly across the blade of the ax. Charlie could hear the file bite into the steel.

"Want to see something, Charlie?" George called.

"Sure!" Charlie ran to George's side after almost tripping over a root that dared interfere with his lunge toward something new.

"This ax so sharp it'll shave the hair right off my arm. Watch." And sure enough as the blade moved across his arm, the thick fair hair just floated away before it. "Want to try it?"

"Yes. Does it hurt?" Before Charlie did it, he looked around, as if he wasn't sure whether he ought to be doing such a thing, as if Gretchen might not approve. But then he sat on the log next to George and carefully pushed the blade of the ax across his forearm. The pale blond hair fell onto the ax blade, just as the long grass did when Matthew went through it with his razor-sharp scythe with the mowing blade. The skin behind the ax was completely smooth, much smoother than the skin of the hogs after they had been scraped at hog-killing time.

"How do you get the ax so sharp, George? When I try to sharpen a sickle, the file just runs over the edge. I can't make it bite."

So George Maupin showed him. The two of them huddled over the ax as George explained how the file was made and how you had to hold it to make it cut into the metal of whatever blade you were sharpening. And how you moved it slow and felt the metal give way to it. And how satisfying it was to test the blade all sharp after only a few strokes.

When he got up from the log, Charlie smiled. But the smile left his face when he glanced down and saw the patch of skin with no hair, smoother even than the skin of the hogs or his father's face after he had shaved in the morning.

MEANWHILE THE HORSES DOZED in the shade of the paradise trees at the woods' edge. When one would twitch off a fly, the other might stir. But usually not. Their ears hung like sails in a calm. When the big oak had been cut into logs, George took loose the singletrees that hung from the hames on the leather collars and after pulling the traces out behind, hooked the singletrees to the doubletree. By this time the two geldings were awake and ready to go. Each had sneezed and swung his head around a little and picked up his ears. While Richie held on to the doubletree, George backed the horses into position and hooked the doubletree to the log.

To Charlie the log looked huge. That evening, in his long and drawn out report to Matthew about his first day logging, he said that the log looked too big for the horses to move at all, let alone drag anywhere. Because in addition to sheer weight, there were the roots of other trees in the way, as well as whole trees. It looked impossible.

When everything was hooked up, George and Richie picked up their peavey hooks, George looped the long steering lines over his arm and hollered "Come up, boys." The two horses put their front legs deep under them, lowered their heads, and leaned into the collars. The log moved. Ahead a root protruded. As the log got to it, George and Richie rolled it sidewise with their peavey hooks just enough to clear the root. They went ten feet before George needed to change the angle so the log would miss a tree. George said, "Whoa," and the horses stopped, eased back off the traces, and seemed to go to sleep again.

Charlie was amazed. The horses and ponies he knew were for pleasure riding or foxhunting and not one would have stood still for this kind of use. Even Leonard Waits's fat workhorse mares were not as quiet as this pair. Charlie said they were like a different kind of animal, said that when they leaned into the traces, you could see all the huge sets of muscles bulge in their shoulders and hindquarters and their nostrils widen. Then they would move — slow, like you would imagine a mountain to move — skidding the huge log forward while George and Richie kept it free of roots with their hooks.

After a few moments' rest George said, "Gee," and used the lines. After three steps to the right the horses were in the clear and lined up to pull again. Of course, Charlie had to get into it at this point, figuring that since he had seen one pull, he was ready to drive the team and help out. George, who like his horses was a gentle soul, had been warned, so he wasn't surprised when Charlie wanted to jump in. And as it turned out, Charlie was a help. He could hold the lines off to the side so George was free to handle the peavey hook with both hands. Charlie knew the commands, and after the second log he could see what needed to happen next. After a while the horses listened to him and he became a part of the crew.

The horses were endlessly interesting to Charlie. The first few days he would walk around them looking at their bodies, trying to understand better how they were put together. He also liked to look at their eyes, which were much bigger than Bat's one eye. He discovered that a horse's eye has a tiny thing like a sea urchin floating in the middle of the pupil. Charlie had never noticed it before. He asked George what the little things were. George said he didn't know, but all horses had them, so he reckoned they were there for some good reason.

Charlie didn't miss a day for the first two weeks of work. He even got Gretchen to pack him a lunch so he could eat with the men, sitting in the shade at the edge of the woods while the horses ate a couple of ears of corn each and dozed. The men ate crackers and canned meat, which Gretchen thought looked rotten, or little wieners, and drank Pepsi-Colas. Charlie had a sandwich and water. Gretchen absolutely refused to buy the canned meat or the wieners or have Charlie drinking what she called soda pop at noon.

At the end of the day, when they were back at the barn and George and Richie had left, Charlie fed the horses their corn. Then he climbed up on Jim's back and felt the movement of the big horse's body as he chewed and swallowed. For the first week, when the horse was finished, Charlie would ride him around the barnyard a few times before turning him and Bill loose in the big pasture for the night. This became a major bone of contention. Matthew didn't approve, and after his admonition appeared not to work, he told Gretchen who told Charlie's father that weekend when he returned from Philadelphia.

At first their conversation did not go well.

"You must stop riding Jim around, Charlie. Surely you understand that. You watch that horse work hard every day. Can't you see he is tired in the evening and needs to rest."

"Yes, but—" This was Charlie's thing, the "but."

"No buts to it," said his father, after they had been around and around a few times. "Just don't ride him.

That's all"—at which point Charlie, uncharacteristically, burst into tears. Mr. Lewis was surprised and later told Gretchen and Matthew, when they had a meeting on the subject, that he had suddenly realized there was more to this than just one of Charlie's whims.

Charlie sobbed and Charles comforted him and then it all came out.

"I want a horse! One that is just mine. To take care of and ride over the whole farm any time I want. And have a saddle and a real bridle, not just an old work bridle. I want Jim. But maybe I want a pony that's easy to get on to. Oh, I don't know . . . I just want a *horse!* I know Jim needs to rest, but I want a horse." This time softly, with more tears.

"I see now," said his father as he hugged Charlie. "We'll talk about it, Charlie. Be patient. Be patient."

Of course, that was a mistake because for Charlie "We'll talk about it" was equal to "Yes we will." His father knew it. But Charlie's anguish had moved him. And without thought he had made a decision.

The three of them—Charles, Gretchen, and Matthew —talked it over. Matthew said fall would be the best time to buy because people would be thinking of the coming winter. Also by that time they might have Charlie convinced that a workhorse was not what he needed. Since he had mentioned a pony, it might even be easy.

Charlie, in part because he was so wrapped up in the logging, readily agreed once the concession was made that he could sit on Jim while the big horse ate his dinner. For some reason, the actual physical contact seemed important to Charlie—seemed to give him comfort.

THEY WORKED ON and the humidity came. The horses sweated standing still. They had to be walked to the creek twice each day for water. Charlie got to ride Jim and lead Bill because that was the easiest way to get the job done. Charlie loved it, even though he was concerned about the horses. Some of the logs were too big for the team to pull, so George hired Leonard to bring his mares to help. But each time the extra team came, George lost his profit on the logs they hauled.

In order to load the logs, the truck was pulled sidewise alongside a high bank and timbers were run from the top of the bank to the log rack. Then the logs were pulled onto the bank and rolled across the timbers onto the truck. Peavey hooks with long handles were used to lever them into position. But as the larger logs were hauled out, it was harder and harder to make up a load with just three men, counting Leonard, all pushing on the peavey hooks.

George was worried. He didn't think he could make the deadline. Always in the past the professor had been easy with such things. But this time he wasn't. There would be no extension. Clarence Flint, who had bought the farm up the valley next to the Smiths, had a bulldozer and had a log skidder coming and was waiting to step in and finish the job. He had a four-horse team to snake the logs out to where the bulldozer could get hold of them and pull them to the truck. So Clarence could make do until the skidder arrived.

GEORGE WENT ONE last time to Silver Hill.

The professor must have been looking out from his study window as George came up the walk, because he was standing at the door when George arrived.

"Hello George. How good to see you," he said in his usual mannerly way. But his face was tense and he was frowning. He must have known George had come to ask for an extension. He walked onto the porch and the two men stood side by side. George, the short one with his powerful body and gruff, bronze face; and the professor, tall and skinny with a face in planes as if cut from rock, and longish gray hair. Normally his face was a beacon of welcome and understanding for the people in the community. But today it was hidden. George said he could see something was awfully wrong. But who was he to ask what? He was just a logger, struggling to make a living in a new world.

The professor drew himself up to his full height. "George," he said, resorting to his most formal language in the embarrassment of his predicament, "it is abhorrent to me that money should take precedence over human needs. As I am sure you know, it has never been my way. But I am constrained by powers beyond my control, and I must have this money by

Labor Day." Here he looked as if he were in literal pain but also very angry, too. He was angered perhaps by his unaccustomed helplessness in the face of some outside situation that, one could guess, would normally have been of no consequence to him whatsoever.

George, who had been looking at the boards on the front porch floor during this speech, looked up. "I can't make it," he said. "I reckon you better get in touch with Clarence. I'll finish this week. Then I'll be gone." He turned away and walked down the old brick walk between the huge boxwoods. As was his custom, he didn't look back.

THE VILLAGE AND CHARLIE and even for a moment Matthew wanted to get up in arms about the whole thing, because Clarence was new and not well liked and George, of course, was a native. Matthew went to the big house the next day and had a talk with the professor. That evening in the store he had nothing to say beyond what the professor had already said. Matthew's face looked grim. Even Charlie could see that although something was wrong, there was absolutely nothing to do about it.

"Charlie, this is the end of it," Matthew had said. "Don't bring it up no more. George's leaving Friday and Clarence's coming Monday, and that's that." And for once Charlie didn't argue. On Friday he stood with his hands at his sides as Jim and Bill were loaded on the neighbor's truck. Bat was there, too. Her ears were cocked. She was watching out of her one eye, gaunt and comic.

When George was ready to leave, Charlie went over and shook hands, which surprised George. He wouldn't have been able to name the last time he had shaken hands with a recently turned eight-year-old.

"So long, Charlie. It's been nice to know you." There was a pause and then George looked straight at Charlie for an instant. "Be careful with Clarence. He ain't like me. And it would be better if you didn't mess with his horses."

Charlie started to ask why, but George had already turned to his truck. It seemed better not to go after the answer. He waved to Richie and George as they pulled out of the barn lot and headed home. Later that day, Matthew said the same thing to Charlie about Clarence.

THERE WERE FOUR of them—three mares and a gelding. They were much smaller than Jim and Bill, and skinnier. Charlie was waiting in the barn lot when they arrived at six o'clock on Monday morning in a big cattle truck. Clarence was driving. There was a man with Clarence whom Charlie had never seen before. Clarence backed up to the bank and jumped out of the truck. He was in a hurry.

"Grab Molly and Paint. I'll get the other two," Clarence whispered at the man with him. When the four horses had been unloaded and walked into the barn, Charlie approached Clarence to say "Good morning," as he had been taught.

Clarence turned to face Charlie head on. His face was flat. His nose barely stuck out at all and the mouth was small and round. He stood over six feet— a baby's face on the body of a giant.

"Now kid," he said in his whispery voice, "I know all about you and I need to tell you something. You stay the hell away from my horses and out of my way, you hear? I'm doing a job here, and I ain't got time for no pissant kid meddling in my business. Now get out of here!"

Charlie was stunned. He always thought of the barn as his, even though it wasn't. Bat was still standing in the lot, watching. Charlie picked up the lead rope, caught Bat, and started up to Silver Hill as fast as he could make the old mule go. He turned her loose in the milk cow field, and Matthew, who emerged from the back porch of the big house, could make out what Charlie was saying, "You stay in here, old mule. Don't you go jumping out and getting messed up with that man, you hear me?" He said this in exactly the same tone as Matthew would have used with him. Matthew smiled and walked over to the boy and put his arm around his shoulders. The two of them stood a moment, looking at the one-eyed mule, beginning to graze.

Charlie asked softly, "How can we keep her from jumping out? She might go over to Clarence."

But before Matthew could answer, they heard the clacking of bulldozer tracks coming from the pond lane. The yellow Allis-Chalmers came into view after running over the cattle guard and breaking loose, as it turned out, two pipes. It was the first time a machine that big had ever been on Silver Hill. It was covered with dust. Clarence didn't have a truck big enough to haul it, so Jake, his son, just drove it cross country on the old logging road, knocking down anything in the way. Some of the trees on that road were twenty years old, because that was the last time it had been used for logging.

"Boy, look at that thing, Matthew. Don't it look neat? I'll bet it can pull a lot of logs out in a big hurry. Don't you think?"

"I reckon so," Matthew replied. "And make a big mess, too."

CHARLIE WAS AFRAID of Clarence and his crew. He stayed away from the barn and the woods, except to watch from the loading chute in the evening as the horses were brought in and fed and then turned out for the night. The second night, when the mare called Molly was slow going into the barn, Clarence whirled around and kicked her in the flank while yelling in his strange voice, "You better get your god-damn ass up in here, mare, before I sure enough kill you."

One day, nearly two years later, Charlie's pony was being willfull, refusing to jump a little jump in the barn lot. It was hot. Charlie was angry, the pony was being stubborn, and suddenly he yelled in a high, strange voice, "You better get your goddamn ass up in here, mare, before I sure enough kill you."

Matthew was hoeing in the garden patch next to the barn lot. He looked up shocked. "Charlie Lewis, what cause you got to talk to that mare like that? I'm half a mind to give you a licking . . ."

But then he saw Charlie's face go white as it always did when something awful happened. He hurried into the lot as the boy slid down from the pony. He was staring somewhere far off and back in time. "What is it, Charlie? What you seeing? Tell me!"

"It was Clarence," he said quietly. "One evening when they were here logging, Molly didn't go into the barn fast enough. He said those words. Those exact words. He kicked her and yelled those words at her. It was awful. I hated it." Fists clenched, he shouted again, "I hated it! I hated it!"

Then Matthew was speaking to him about it being bearable because Charlie knew better, knew enough to cry. He swayed back and forth as he held the boy in his arms, until Charlie stopped sobbing. It was almost nothing, really, compared to what else happened.

TUESDAY OF THE second week, when the big power skidder still hadn't come, and Clarence was getting behind, Charlie noticed a bullwhip hanging from the collar of Molly's harness. It was black leather and the handle was thick. Once in the village, Charlie had seen Jimmy Price showing off with one like it to some little kids. Charlie had been fascinated. It made a loud noise when Jimmy cracked it. The handle was heavy. Jimmy said it would knock you out if he hit you with it. If a lot of black leather on a black handle could be said to be ugly, this was ugly.

Charlie ran for Matthew who, because it was early morning, was in the milking barn. "Clarence has a bullwhip hanging off of Molly's collar. He's going to whip her with it. I know he is. You have to do something. Quick! Now!"

As always when Charlie came in during milking, Matthew looked up and pushed back his leather baseball cap. "Charlie, that horse belongs to him. I can't go in there telling a man what to do with his property. He'd got to do something pretty awful before the law would come. Laying a whip on her ain't awful enough. There just ain't nothing to do so far."

That evening as he watched from the chute, Charlie could see the welts on Molly's back. They looked like tracks of black hair through the red dust on her dark hide. He could see the welts on the others, too, but Molly's were the worst. Clarence was in a rage, yelling in his whispery voice to no one in particular, "If that goddamn son-of-a-bitching skidder don't come quick, I'm going to end up just like that shithead George— in a hole." And then to his son, Tommy, "These goddamn horses got to work tomorrow. We got to get caught up. If that lazy-ass Molly don't pull tomorrow, I'll knock her head off."

In the morning Charlie left early, before Clarence and his crew were even at the barn. He circled around behind the summerhouses to where they were logging. The bulldozer was parked at the edge of the woods. Charlie hadn't been there since George had left. The place was a mess. The earth was gouged out where the bulldozer had made ruts while pulling out the logs. The laps were left where they had been cut instead of pulled to the open and piled for burning. Cans and bottles were all over the area where the men ate lunch. The woods looked dirty.

Charlie crawled behind a huge fallen tree. Time passed. The men and horses came and began work. Charlie said later that from the beginning Clarence was furious at his two sons and the other white man he didn't recognize, telling them over and over what they already knew—that the skidder was not coming for another week. The horses felt the strain. They would jump sideways at Clarence's slightest move. Even the air was full of tension. High billowing thunderheads slowly moved in from the west, above Burdens Mountain.

The bullwhip hung coiled on Molly's collar. Charlie watched. The logs that they were skidding out of the woods were the huge ones. The four horses struggled. Clarence seldom let them rest. Then a really big log caught on a root. Without turning to see what had stopped the log, Clarence jerked the whip from Molly's harness, stepped back to get the distance, and began to whip the four horses, cursing them steadily.

Molly was the smallest. She gave up first. Clarence slowly coiled the whip in his left hand, keeping the handle in his right. With a horrible sound, he lunged at the mare and started beating her in the head with the handle, his voice raised to a shriek, his baby face contorted in rage.

The instant he hit her in the eye the first time, Charlie was up and running at him, screaming, "Stop!" —his loud voice already clouded with hysteria and tears, covering the hundred feet before Clarence was aware of what was going on. Charlie threw himself at Clarence's arm, but he was too late. The butt of the handle had knocked out Molly's right eye like breaking an egg.

Clarence turned and shook the boy off his arm. When he realized who his assailant was, he even smiled as he recoiled the whip. "You just stay there, you little shitass, and I'm going to teach you to mess with me. Thinking you're so high and mighty with that damn professor—him and that nigger you go around with. Well, he ain't here to take care of you now."

Charlie was still on the ground, transfixed by the language and the horror of Molly's eye. Clarence got the distance and raised the whip. Tommy hurled himself at his father, "No, Pap, if you hit the little son of a bitch, they'll call the law on us, and you'll go to jail and they'll take everything we own." By this time Tommy had hold of his father's arms. So the stroke of the whip was deflected.

Charlie got up and ran toward home, screaming for

Gretchen and Matthew. He found her first. By the time the two of them found Matthew, Gretchen was nearly hysterical herself because she couldn't imagine what had happened. It wasn't until they were all in the professor's study that Matthew started to get the story. At the part about Molly's eye, Gretchen started to sob uncontrollably, until she looked up and saw the pain on the professor's face, as if he himself had been there and let it happen.

The professor called the sheriff and gave him the gist of the thing. Twenty-five minutes later, Sheriff Cook came in the lane in a cloud of dust with the siren on. He had two deputies with him. He was very excited. Everyone knew Clarence Flint.

"Do you reckon he has a gun?" asked the sheriff. They all looked at Charlie who shook his head no. No one questioned how Charlie would know. They just went. Matthew said by the time the car had bounced across the field the deputies had out the sawed-off shotguns, ready for anything.

All they found was Clarence and his two sons. The fourth man had run. Clarence was sitting on a log, like he was waiting for them, elbows on knees, chin in hands. He looked exhausted. His child's face looked smooth and blank, like polished stone. The two boys looked as if they wanted more than anything in the world to go home. The four horses were exactly where they had stopped. Molly had her head almost to the ground. Her ears were pulled back in pain. Every few seconds she shook her head. The fluid from her eye had run down her cheek like she had shed a monstrous tear. Sheriff Cook picked up the whip and for a second looked like he would use it. He threw it to a deputy and motioned for Clarence to get in the car.

"Now you boys listen to me and listen good," said the sheriff to Clarence's sons. "You take them horses down to the barn and get the harness off them and clean up that mare's eye. Stay there until the veterinary comes. And do what he says. And God Almighty help you if you run off. Because if you do I will hunt you down like dogs . . ." He struggled for composure. He said later that never before in his life as sheriff had he wanted to hurt someone. He said the picture of that mare with her head hanging down to the ground would stay with him for the rest of his life. And Shirley Cook had seen some pretty awful things in his day.

The deputies stayed in the car with Clarence while Sheriff Cook and Matthew went back into the house to talk to the professor and call Doc White, the veterinarian. Gretchen and Charlie were still there. Mrs. James and Sally had made tea. The professor had put a little brandy in the tea—for Charlie, too. Matthew said they looked like ghosts they were so pale. Mr. Lewis wouldn't be home till Friday night. Maybe they should spend the night at Silver Hill.

Shirley Cook called the vet and told his assistant what was needed. She said Dr. White would leave town right away, be there in thirty minutes.

Matthew and Professor James and the sheriff stood

on the front porch. "You know the law, Professor, you teach it. All I can do is take him down to the court house and yell at him," said the sheriff. "I can't lock him up for knocking his own mare's eye out. Anyway, he would say that it was an accident and the two boys would back him up. He might even try to get Charlie for assault." He shook his head in disgust. "I swear to God, it was about the cruelest thing I ever seen. What can we do with the mare?"

"Send her to Miss Alice Jackson," said the professor. "You know how she loves animals, and now that she has let her cow go, she has room. Matthew can arrange it. I'll take care of the feed and vet." He paused. "But I still have the problem of getting that damn timber sold . . ."

The way they worked it out—law or no law—was that the Flints would go back to work the next day. An off-duty deputy would check on them twice a day. The boys would be all right because, curiously, they were more scared of the law than they were of Clarence. Matthew would supervise the feeding of the three remaining horses, morning and evening. Clarence agreed to the plan because he knew that if he didn't, he'd never get another day's worth of work in that county. His sullen baby face never changed, though; he just spat out yes. And as planned, Molly would be sent to Miss Alice who was lonely and would be happy to nurse her back to health.

• • •

MATTHEW RETURNED TO the house to tell Gretchen and Charlie what was going to happen. While he was explaining, the sheriff left and the professor started in the front door. Mrs. James was waiting for him. Matthew said that for the first time in his life he saw them have sharp words. The professor even raised his voice a little and Matthew heard him say, "Yes, damn it, we'll get the money in time."

Gretchen and Charlie went home the next morning after spending the night in the big house. Sally made a wonderful dinner and Mrs. James was kind. Charlie didn't go near the barn or the woods. He spent a lot of time with the old mule. He was seen staring at her face. For a week he hardly spoke. Everyone worried. Charlie talking nonstop was sometimes a nuisance, but Charlie silent was unsettling. The skidder arrived in time to get the timber out, so the professor would get his money by Labor Day.

Molly slowly recovered. Doc White eventually took out the eye and sewed her eyelid shut, and she was fine—just like old Bat, except she didn't have any eyeball at all. She stayed with Miss Alice because no one wanted her to go back to Clarence and he was afraid to insist.

A month passed and Charlie still was nearly silent. Matthew wondered what else was wrong. Charlie began to come to the little milking barn in the morning and evening. He would sit silent in the corner while the milk swished into the bucket. He had always liked milking time. He liked the smell of the cow and the sound of her chewing, Matthew's breathing, and in the summer the buzz of a wasp. One evening, after they were finished and were walking up the path to the gate, Bat was there, facing them. Charlie was in front. He stopped for a moment and then began to shake. Matthew barely had time to put the bucket down before Charlie whirled around into his arms. "Tell me how it happened! Tell me. Did Leonard hit her? Did he beat her? Tell me."

For an instant Matthew didn't understand. The boy had gone wild. He tried to restrain him. When Charlie yelled out Leonard's name, Matthew looked up at old Bat and made the connection.

He grabbed Charlie shoulders. Hard. He put his face close to his. "Charlie! You stop. I can't tell you nothing if you don't shut up." Then louder, "Hush! You hear me?" And shook him. The boy looked at him, at his eyes, with their bloodshot whites and pupils like dark pools. Eyes he had known for what seemed like his whole life. He stopped.

"Turn around, Charlie! Look at her! What you see!"

"I see," he gasped, because Matthew had such a hold on him, "I see a milky-looking eye that's blind. Blind! How did it happen? Tell me!"

"Go close. What else you see, Charlie? . . . What?"

Charlie peered at the eye. "I see a scar on the milky part where something went into it. What was it?"

Matthew let him go and the boy turned again to face him.

"One time when she was a foal," Matthew said,

"she was running in the pasture. You know that growed-up pasture behind old man Waits's house? It was worse then. But there was grass in it, and the mare needed to eat to raise her foal. There was a lot of black locust in that field. Leonard saw it happen. Saw her slip and run right into a tree with locust stobs sticking out all over it. And drove one right into her eye. And her swinging her head back and forth in pain. Leonard's daddy wanted to put her down. Said it would just get infected and cost money. But Leonard nursed her back without no veterinary. She growed up and they named her Bat and she been working ever since. That's all. That's what happened."

There was silence.

"You never told me."

"You never did ask. How can I tell you what you don't ask?" He paused. "Now Charlie," said Matthew talking his slowest, "you listen to me. You might go through your whole life and never again meet nobody like Clarence Flint. But if you do, there's one damn sure thing, you'll know who he is and shun him. You never did think Leonard was like Clarence, did you?"

There was silence.

Then Charlie slowly shook his head. He looked worn out from the tension of the story. The old mule stirred. Charlie turned to look at her. The boy had stopped shaking and even though his back was to him, Matthew felt him smile. It was a mild evening. Abruptly the old mule flopped her comic ears forward and lowered her head. Charlie walked up to her and stared at her blind, milky eye.

"That scar always been there," said Matthew. "You just ain't ever seen it before. But then again, I reckon you ain't ever had the need before."

The Pony

SHE CAME FROM THE Price family's little hardpan farm, five ridges back from the barn at the Corn House. She was gray, flea-bitten gray, which meant she was white with little black specks scattered over her body. And because of our red-clay soil, what you actually saw varied from light pink in the summer to reddish brown in the winter. The shade of red was governed by rainfall. In times of drought or summer heat, when her coat was short, she was almost her natural color, almost white. In the winter, with a long coat and rain, she would turn the vivid color of the soil and stay that way for months. In the beginning, Mr. Lewis tried to get Charlie to groom the little mare regularly. The idea was to keep her looking clean, not reddish brown or pink. The effort was, of course, a failure. Hot water and soap wouldn't have done it, let alone what Charlie's daddy called elbow grease. She was indivisible from the land. Her name was Tricksey.

Everyone agreed the name was awful. Charlie wanted to rename her Fleet Foot because it fit with his ideas about what he was going to do with her. But it didn't stick. She came Tricksey and many years later she died Tricksey. Almost immediately Charlie began referring to her as "the pony." And that is what she became in everyday use.

The purchase of the pony was the result of the promise given during the summer. His father had meant it when he agreed that in the fall Charlie would get a pony, when horses and ponies were for sale at the right price because cold weather meant hay and feed and not everyone could carry livestock over the winter.

Charlie had seen Jimmy Price riding her around the village and announced he thought she would do just fine. Jimmy had even let Charlie try her in the lot behind the store. Jimmy was an accepted authority on horses because he had that mare named Princess, who would lie down and roll over on command. Tricksey was no Princess, but Jimmy held out the vague hope that she might be taught to at least lie down. Tricksey did respond to Charlie by doing more or less what he wanted. She circled obediently around the lot, stopping and going forward on command. Also, she was short enough that he could climb on her from the ground. So Charlie fastened his desire on Tricksey.

Matthew couldn't see any reason why not. Everyone knew the Price family. Old Aaron Price was a blacksmith—mainly horseshoeing, not ironwork—whose family had been around nearly as long as the Jameses, so you knew who you were buying from.

The negotiation for her purchase was complex. Messages were sent via Jimmy. In the beginning, Aaron didn't really want to sell her. It wasn't that he needed her. He didn't, but he collected horses the way Luke Henry collected hounds. He must have had ten horses and ponies on the twenty-five-acre hardpan red-clay plot that he called a farm. In addition to shoeing, he was a part-time horse trader who didn't really trade horses very often because he seemed to like them all and want to keep them.

The Price's house and barns were made of logs, the fences of field-pine poles. The place looked like something out of old times, like a little fortified compound. There was no plumbing, and water was dipped from the dug well right behind the kitchen. There were three cows and three steers and the usual hog pen over the hill behind the house. Add the money from Aaron's shoeing, and they were self-sufficient.

The lane into the compound was solid red clay, between banks that were nearly as high as the cab of Matthew's old black pickup. Charles Lewis wondered aloud how the Prices got in and out in bad weather.

"They leave their truck out to the hard road and walk," said Matthew. "No way on earth you going to get a truck up this lane if it's wet."

Aaron was trying to retire. That meant he wanted Jimmy to take up the slack of the shoeing so Aaron could sit on the porch and chew, take a pull at the jug every once in a while, and look out at the stock—and maybe buy and sell some horses. Jimmy didn't necessarily mind the work. It was just that he liked all kinds of other things as well—horse shows in the spring and summer and livestock sales in the winter, and just plain wandering around the countryside visiting with people. But Jimmy had real talent. At sixteen, he was already a master horseshoer. His work was in demand.

Aaron was sitting on the front porch. As Charles and Matthew and Charlie approached, he spat over the porch rail and smiled his nearly toothless grin and said come on up and have a seat. Matthew did the talking while Charles looked bored and Charlie fidgeted.

Finally Aaron summed it up. "Well, Matthew, I never did really want to sell that little mare and $150 don't sound like enough, but"—here he spat conclusively over the rail—"I'll think on it and let you know.

"Nice to meet you, Mr. Lewis. Charlie, you sure are growing like a weed. That little mare *would* suit you . . ."

Back in the truck Charlie talked a mile a minute as if to make up for the time lost while Matthew and old Aaron hemmed and hawed.

"When can I take her home, Matthew?"

"Don't you go getting all hotted up over it, Charlie. That old man don't do nothing in a hurry."

"How long? A week?"

"Do you think he'll sell her at all?" Charles asked. "Mr. Price didn't seem anxious to me."

"Don't you be fooled by that, Mr. Lewis," Matthew replied. "You can bet your life Miz Price was back in the kitchen listening, and no sooner we was gone she come at him about getting rid of that pony cause they had bills to pay and how he didn't need her nohow . . . No, he'll let her go. We just might have to wait a week or two."

Two DAYS LATER the Price's log house caught fire and burned to the ground along with the main barn, which was only forty feet from the back door. Everyone got out, people and livestock. The three older boys had already moved out and were starting families, so at the time of the fire only Jimmy and Aaron and the old lady were at home. The community rallied round. The three humans moved into the vacant cottage at the back of Mill Creek Farm. The cows and steers were sold and the horses split up between Silver Hill and Mill Creek. Much to Charlie's disgust, Tricksey—because she was a mare and the mares were kept together—went to Mill Creek.

And then, just like out of the Bible, Aaron had a heart attack and, the day after that, died. Everyone said it was the strain of losing the place where he had lived all his life.

Whatever the reason, Mrs. Price was now in charge. She was an old-fashioned lady who was tall and upright and wore long dresses and a sun bonnet, summer and winter. She had put up with Aaron and Jimmy's horse foolishness for years, but the morning after the funeral, she marched into the post office and told Mr. Dudley that the horses were for sale—cheap. And please tell Matthew when you see him to come and get that pony mare, and $150 was just fine. This scene was watched with interest by everyone in the store/post office. Normally Mrs. Price only came into the store to buy groceries. The rest of the time she sat in the truck while Jimmy and Aaron stood around inside and talked.

But not now. It was as if she had been waiting all her life to step into this situation. Within two days the horses were sold except Princess. Mrs. Price had made arrangements with a cousin to rent a house in a village ten miles north of us. Jimmy suddenly had a new outlook on life because his mama told him if he didn't spend his time shoeing horses, Princess would go somewhere else along with the rest of the useless horses. She meant it. And Jimmy knew it.

So the deal was struck for Tricksey. And for another fifty dollars, a flat English saddle and a bridle were thrown in. The money was delivered. All that was left was to get the pony home from the back pasture at Mill Creek. Of course, Charlie wanted to ride her home but Gretchen put her foot down. After all, the boy really knew nothing about riding. She just wouldn't hear of it. Matthew had not been on a horse since he was a little boy. And, anyway, he was too big for that pony. Or so he said.

That left Charlie's father, who quickly realized he was stuck with it. Sitting on the pony, his feet were only a foot from the ground. He had himself not sat on a horse or pony since he was a boy at camp. Matthew and Charlie watched as Charles made his way across the field, headed for the Corn House. Charles had one hand on the reins and the other on the top of his head holding down his hat as if in wind. But there was no wind. Just a late October afternoon with the leaves in full color and the air mild and dry.

"Hurry, Matthew!" Charlie said. "We need to be at home just as soon as he gets there."

"There ain't no hurry. It'll take him an hour and even my old truck can make it in ten minutes. No hurry."

They stood next to the white fence. Matthew leaned on the top board, his black hands resting lightly on the whitewashed oak. Charlie watched through the second board as the little mare and his father disappeared over the hill.

A young red-tailed hawk came across the woods from the steep hill behind them, lightly riding the air. He was young enough that his body was still white with dark spots. He whistled his harsh "keeeeer" and for a second halted his journey and looked down.

"Look, Matthew, he's hunting. How can he do that? I mean just stop in midair like that."

Before Matthew could answer, the hawk dove like a rock, falling into a clump of broom sage. He paused and spread his wings. His red tail feathers were the color of the clay soil. When he rose up into the air again, he was clutching a vole with one foot. Then he was gone, over the hill and gone.

Hawks were coming back now that the number of people keeping chickens steadily declined. They were no longer shot on sight. Charlie took them for granted, while Matthew was always surprised to see one after the long years when there had been none. Gradually they were becoming part of the backdrop of our lives, the sound of their cry part of the rhythm of our world.

"How did he know where the vole was?" Charlie asked. "He just stopped all that way off the ground and then dove. How did he know, Matthew?"

"I don't know, Charlie. I just don't know. When I growed up, they'd been shot out to where you never saw one. I never had a chance to watch when I was little. Maybe if there had of been a lot of them to look at, I might have seen how they did it. Maybe you can figure it out what with there being plenty to watch." And then he said abruptly, "Let's go. Time to be home and get ready for that pony." Charlie's mind turned away from the hawk's eyesight and came back to the pony.

"Yes, let's hurry. Come on!" and headed for the truck.

EVERYONE WAS LINED UP in the lane in front of the Corn House, when Mr. Lewis came over the hill at Silver Hill and started down the lane to home. First there was Gretchen, looking slightly apprehensive but happy that Charlie would have a horse of his own. She thought of the pony as a horse because she had never been around them growing up, so a horse was a horse no matter what the size. Matthew and Charlie completed the human delegation, with Matthew standing between Charlie and his mother. Next was Bat the one-eyed mare mule, Charlie's friend despite the fact that an eight-year-old boy seldom if ever had a mule for a friend—at least as far as any of us knew. And finally Brown, an amiable, longhaired mongrel dog of that color who belonged to a family in the village but spent most of his time on the road scavenging. One of his ears stood straight up and the other flopped over, as if he could understand questions and answers at the same time. He had a regular route and today was his day to be at the Corn House.

As Mr. Lewis came down the hill, obviously in some discomfort from the long, unaccustomed ride, Bat cocked her head, flopped her ears forward, and produced an appropriate bellow of welcome that frightened the pony, who whirled around, nearly leaving Charlie's daddy behind, and started back the way she had come. It only took a couple of strides for Mr. Lewis to regain control, but it was typical. Over time, the pony was to gain some local fame for independence, and almost unloading Mr. Lewis before he had even got her home was her first shot. Charlie was beside himself with excitement.

"Get off, Daddy. Get off so I can ride." This even before Mr. Lewis had recovered from almost being ditched. Then he was down and Charlie was up, pulling at the stirrup leathers to make them a couple of feet shorter. But it didn't work. There weren't enough holes. Charlie tensed all over and looked up with something like panic in his eyes. Matthew said later that he had never seen a kid tie himself in such knots over a pony.

"Now what, Matthew? They won't work. There aren't enough holes." Charlie, of course, turned to Matthew in this time of emergency.

"Come on, Charlie, there's a harness punch up to the shop at the big house. I'll punch the holes."

A little later the two of them were at the top of the hill in front of the garage, Matthew with the punch and the leathers pulled out, intent on the task, and Charlie looking down at Matthew's hands, his eyes locked onto the leather and the old rusty punch, with the slanting October light coming over his shoulder, illuminating the pony's head as she dozed on her feet, ears relaxed, uninterested.

When the stirrups were the right length, Charlie pushed his feet into them and stood up, holding on to the pony's mane and looking around as if he were seeing the familiar scene for the first time, smiling as the yellow light fell across his pale features. When he sat back into the saddle, he looked from Matthew's smile to the ends of the stirrup leathers, which were so long they fell beneath the pony's belly.

"Cut them off, Matthew. They look dumb hanging down like that. Cut them off."

"Now Charlie," he said, "one of these days you going to grow up and need those leathers long." Here he paused and said, no longer smiling, "Surely you'll need these here leathers. Don't you dare cut them off. Here's how to fold them up into the keeper straps . . ."

That evening after he had taken his first ride and put the pony away in the barn to eat an ear of corn, Charlie hurried up the hill to the big house, looking for Matthew.

"Why, Charlie, what you limping about? What happened?"

The boy was livid. "That damn pony kicked me! That's what."

Matthew said it was the first time he'd ever seen Charlie angry like that. And certainly it was the first time he'd heard him use bad language. Matthew smiled as he told the story to Fred Henry that evening in the store.

"Fred, that boy was mad. He was so fussed it took a while to get the story out of him. What happened was he led the pony into the barn and tied her next to the manger and went to get her an ear of corn. I reckon he felt like he needed to feed her something after the ride. He thought it would be a nice thing to do. So over to the barrel he goes and pulls out an ear and starts back to her. Now of course that pony ain't used to eating grain, so she gets all excited and puts her ears back and starts switching her tail. Charlie don't know no better, so he walks behind her to get to the manger. And, whap, she kicks him right in the knee and knocks him down. Hit his funny bone. That boy flew hot! He jumps up and turns around to her and raises his hand. He's still standing right behind her, mind you. Well, she slaps her ears down again and cocks a leg. By this time Charlie has figured out that this pony ain't no workhorse. And not only that, she got a mind all her own and won't put up with any foolishness from nobody. He still has a mind to take a poke at her with a broom handle. But after what he seen Clarence do to that mare last summer, he ain't going to be mean to no horse no matter what. So he's stuck. He thinks it ain't fair. That pony didn't have no cause to kick him, seeing as how he was being kind, not mean. 'So why did she do it?' he asks. Well, what's to say? That she's just a pony mare and that's the way she is? Anyway, that's what I told him. One thing for sure, though, that boy ain't going around that mare's back end again without he looks at her ears first."

They smiled at Charlie's dilemma as they always did. Even at eight, Charlie had grown deep into the community.

FROM THE BEGINNING, relations with the pony were strained. For starters and much to the amusement of everyone in the store, Charlie had been told by his father that he was not to canter the pony until he had had her for at least six months. It was Charlie's daddy's way of having Charlie start his riding career slowly. Of course, Charlie being Charlie, that didn't work. He cantered everywhere from the beginning and as a result didn't learn to post to the trot until he was eleven. But when the pony didn't want to canter, which was nearly always, she had a way of jerking along at a gait that was technically a canter but was in fact a very rough way to ride indeed. Finally exasperation overtook Charlie's pacifism toward horses and he cut a switch from a maple behind the barn. The next time the pony did her herky-jerky gait, he was ready and slapped her good behind the saddle with the switch. The results were deeply satisfying. Suddenly the pony was floating over the ground in a lovely canter that was completely comfortable to ride. It had taken Charlie until November to figure this out, so there had been a lot of rough riding in between.

Another problem was catching her up from the field. The field in this case was over a hundred acres, because when Silver Hill had ceased to be a real working farm, the cross fences were let go and the gates left open. As a result, the four original fields became one. There were groves of trees interspersed throughout the field along with two creeks. The whole thing had gone wild. The result was occasionally rented out for pasture, but even the outside fences were going bad, so most people didn't think it was worth it to have to chase cows that even inside the fences had only broom sage to eat.

The morning after he got her home, Charlie turned the pony loose in the field. She disappeared for two days. He walked and walked and called and called. The third day, as he crossed the first ridge, he saw her standing next to the creek at the foot of the hill. There were some small walnut trees growing next to the stream alongside a clump of multiflora rose and honeysuckle, long past blooming. She was standing with her back end to him, inside the tangle of vines, slowly swishing the late fall flies with her tail. Had it not been for the tail, he would have never seen her. Following Jimmy Price's instructions, he rushed back to the barn and got an ear of corn. He circled around to get in front of her and whistled the horse-calling whistle and held out his hand with the corn. She raised her head, looked at him, and trotted off next to the creek on a path cut nearly a foot deep by hundreds of cattle hooves. Then she disappeared into a pine thicket at the head of the stream.

Charlie followed, calling her name. He'd never been in the thicket before. He walked the path carefully, looking down. The thicket consisted of cedars interspersed with field pine. Twenty-five feet in, it suddenly opened into a clearing with three large oaks in the middle. The clearing was more than an acre. It startled Charlie to break suddenly into the open after the prickers of the cedars and the twisting of the path. He looked up.

The pony was standing beneath one of the oaks, facing him, ears up, looking right at him, still almost white from the dry summer. She was surrounded completely by a sea of white, bleached bones. Dozens of bones. There must have been thirty cow skulls lying in the clearing. But not just cows'. Charlie recognized the elongated skulls of horses and mules, and wide horse hooves and the unmistakably round and narrow hooves of mules. They were scattered around haphazardly. Charlie recognized some of the other bones. The hipbones looked huge and circular and the long bones of the legs were easy to recognize. Some of the rib cages were still intact, but mostly the ribs had been strewn about by the creatures that had eaten the flesh from them, leaving sections of vertebrae in piles. The thick wall of cedars and pines kept out the breeze. It was still, the day cloudy and cool with the hint of winter. The pony looked at him. Charlie looked at the bones and then at the pony.

Of course he'd heard of it, the boneyard. But he'd never known where it was exactly. This was the most remote place on the farm. No one came here except to drag a dead cow or horse or mule, and because the land was no longer farmed it had been years since this place had last been used. He'd had no previous interest in it. But it was different now. The boneyard was her hiding place. She had found it by crossing and recrossing the hundred acres, grazing at night, her head never far from the ground, searching for the best grasses and the places humans seldom went, until she found the one place where people didn't venture at all. And knew immediately that she had escaped, until, as horses will, she led Charlie to the very place where in the end she could have lost him.

He didn't know the names of all the bones, but he knew her name. He put out his hand with some of the corn kernels in it and spoke to her. She let him catch her. She ate the hard kernels of field corn from his hand while he snapped the lead onto her halter. He led her very carefully along the little path so they wouldn't trip on the bones, across the clearing and out of the thicket.

Later, when Charlie told it in his dramatic way, he said he was surprised the pony hadn't been afraid in there with all those dead bones. But Robert Paine rolled his bloodshot eyes in his intensely black face and said in derision, "Charlie, you do make things more than what they is. That pony got better sense than that. She knows ain't nothing living-dead in there. She knows they's nothing to them bones. They's all dried up just like in the Bible. Anyway, she don't care nothing about dead things. You the one—not her."

It was a strange outburst. Robert had never paid much attention to Charlie. But by this time Charlie's passions were becoming of interest to us. Not many eight-year-olds wonder what a pony knows about death. It was just strange. And Charlie's ideas seemed to strike some deep resentment in Robert that never left him. Not until Charlie was gone from the place. Maybe not even then.

Winter came and it snowed—not a lot, just enough to turn the roads to mud and the pony to her deepest reddish brown. The days grew too short for riding. Sometimes the only way Charlie knew she was still in the field was that in the evenings, when he took her feed to the foot of the pear tree on the other side of the creek behind the barn, the previous day's ration would be gone.

One Saturday in December when it was clear, Charlie walked over the hill to the boneyard wondering if she would be there. She was. This time she looked completely out of place. There was a little snow on the ground, just enough to make the place look whiter than usual. The pony was standing beneath her tree, covered with clay from end to end—in complete contrast to her surroundings. Even so, she was like a harbinger, as if the red clay in her coat somehow brought an earnest of spring into that white, bone-laden place.

OLD BAT THE MULE spent the winter in the little field behind the house at Silver Hill where the milk cow lived. Bat liked to be near Matthew in bad weather because she knew he would slip her a coffee can of cow feed each evening. She loved the fine-ground feed and would snort and cough as she ate it. Charlie and Matthew thought it amazing that a twenty-five-year-old one-eyed mule would love dairy feed.

Brown the mutt cruised through on a regular basis because he knew Gretchen would give him scraps. The Corn House was tight and the radiators were nice to touch on a cold morning. Charlie's father came home from Philadelphia on the weekends and Gretchen minded the Corn House and read. Sometimes in the afternoon she had tea with Professor James in the front parlor of the big house. Charlie had school, which he seemed to like all right. And old Bat, when she had jumped out of the pasture, waited for him at the bus stop. We got used to the picture of the two of them trudging up the lane to Silver Hill on a winter's afternoon.

The next time Charlie searched for the pony she wasn't in the boneyard. From then on he only saw her when she was eating her hay in the morning as he left for school. She had never had so much to eat in her life, and with the mud caked into her thick winter coat she would be warm no matter how bad the weather.

Sometimes Charlie saw the red-tailed hawk in the afternoon. He would hear the whistle and look up to see the young hawk riding the air. But he never saw him dive again that winter. He didn't know whether this hawk was the one he'd seen that afternoon in the back pasture at Mill Creek. Charlie liked to hear the whistle, the harsh, descending "keeeeer." The hawk was a sentinel, a watcher. Charlie wondered of what. No one he asked was sure.

Our lives were snug and in order, waiting for the winter to be over.

THE HAWK DECLARED the spring. In late April, Charlie, who would be nine that summer, saw the red tail hunting high above the field next to the lane into Silver Hill. He and Bat were walking in together after school. In the beginning, whenever he saw the hawk, he waited for him to dive. But, as time went on, the experience at Mill Creek faded and Charlie no longer waited in suspense for the sudden fall of the hawk. So when it happened that day, he was caught off guard. He told Matthew that the suddenness of it took his breath away. The hawk landed not twenty feet from him and Bat. This time when the red tail spread his wings over the clump of broom sage, he also spread his tail, his vivid reddish-brown tail, so that half of him seemed to disappear into the ground. As usual when something exciting happened, Charlie was in a knot. He reached up and grabbed Bat's halter. But the mule was impassive. Except for greetings, things had to be out of whack to get her attention.

At the beginning of May the pony began to shed her winter coat. Charlie was riding again, and Matthew had shown him how to take the rough metal curry-comb to the thick hair and make it fall out in clumps. As a result by the middle of the month she was gleaming. Even if there was rain she only stayed mud-colored for a day or so. She would roll in the winter grass and finish what Charlie and the brushes and curry had begun. She changed from the color of the clay to almost white again.

THE DAY IT HAPPENED began as any other chilly but clear spring Saturday morning. After breakfast Charlie walked to the barn, got an ear of corn, and went to find the pony. Brown was wandering around, hoping for a handout. Old Bat looked down on the Corn House from in front of the garage at the big house, and every imaginable plant and animal was engaged in leaping into life. The red tail cruised over head. Charlie heard his whistle and looked up.

The pony was in the boneyard, looking her whitest. For once she let him walk right up to her. Charlie led the pony down the hill to the barn. Old Bat hee-hawed her greeting from the other hill and Charlie smiled.

He led the pony around to the front of the barn. Just as he was about to step across the concrete threshold, Gretchen called from the house telling him to come right now and get a sweater. The tone of voice was clear. He had better come right now. So once in the barn he hurriedly turned the pony around and tied the end of the lead rope to the ring next to the door, leaving four feet of it dangling. Then he hooked the low half door from the outside. He was in a hurry. It was time to go riding, sweater or no sweater.

The rest of it came in a rush. Just as he was coming down the stairs with his sweater, Charlie heard the crash and knew what had happened. Not in his thinking mind, but he knew just the same, knew that he had made the rope too long. Then he was running, dropping the sweater in his haste. As he rounded the loading chute, he saw from the corner of his eye old Bat at the foot of the hill, walking toward him. Brown, too, had heard the strange noise and was coming in a hurry.

She was upside down on the outside of the barn with the door still closed and the rope lead still tied inside, short enough that it held her head half way up the door as she thrashed and thrashed, her hooves hitting the door like sledge hammers.

Charlie knew he could not go close enough to free her. Her feet were dangerous beyond any willfulness on her part. In fear and anger and with all her strength, she was trying to free herself. Her eyes were unseeing.

From high above the barn, the red tail whistled. Brown went half crazy. He bounced around the pony on stiff legs, darting at her, barking—suddenly caught up by some deep part of his nature that saw her as a grass eater, helpless, prey. Charlie screamed at him.

She had gashed her side on the sharp edge of one of the old boards on the door as she had jumped out. Blood was mingling with the dirt as she struggled. Then the rope broke and the pony leaped up. She stood stiff, legs apart, her tail swishing back and forth, spreading the blood along her flanks, turning them a dull red.

The dog came to his senses and Charlie approached the pony. She raised her head and looked as if she would let him catch her. But Charlie hesitated as he reached for what was left of the lead rope. She jerked back and trotted off around the barn and up the hill, still swishing her tail. The boy followed, calling her name. But she didn't stop. He knew where she was going. He could have taken a shortcut and arrived before she did. Instead he followed her along the old path. She slowed to a walk, but he made no effort to catch up.

Once in the boneyard she would go to her tree and turn to face him. He would approach her with his left hand outstretched, holding a little grass that he had picked up along the way, patting the grass with his right hand, calling her name. The bleached bones in the clearing would be shining in the late morning sun. Her ears would be forward, the rope from her halter hanging to the ground, her tail steadily swishing the blood along her flanks. There would be a breathless pause. Then he would reach for the rope. At the last moment, she would pull back. Just beyond his reach. Again and again. Ever receding, as if into a dream. And the young hawk circling overhead would be watching through mysterious eyes.

Backfire

IT BEGAN THAT SPRING as a whisper, a dry rustling of last year's leaves across our landscape. There was dust everywhere. The corn came up, but by the first of June it stopped growing. Sunrise and sunset turned red. A sudden spurt of rain in late June helped the corn shoot up a little more—but that was all. The first cutting of hay was the last one for the season. People began to worry.

The pastures at Silver Hill were all broom sage, but in the spring they usually turned green for a while with the new growth. But not that year. By August the state began to put signs along the roads warning of fire hazard.

All the important people in my life were gardeners: Matthew grew vegetables, and Will, my godfather priest, and Gretchen, my mother, grew flowers. It was more than a hobby for all of them. Somehow the growth of the plants had a hold on them. They measured a part of their lives by how the gardens were doing. By imitation, so did I.

It was during that first summer of the drought that I heard the prayer for rain. And from then on—because the drought seemed to last forever—I heard the prayer every Sunday: "Send us, we beseech thee, in this our necessity, such moderate rain and showers, that we may receive the fruits of the earth to our comfort, and to thy honor . . ." In times of trouble or doubt, the words still play in my mind, as if that lack of rain summed up all trouble; and colored Aunt Millie somehow had the last word when in response to the question how she felt would say, "Well, it ain't rained yet. But the Lord will provide in due time. But it don't feel like anytime soon."

People began to worry about their wells and springs. By the second summer, some went dry. Not ours, though. Our spring had been developed to supply water to the locomotives that stopped at the depot. It was the most powerful spring in the area. So there was plenty of water, particularly after the steam locomotives went out. There was even enough that Matthew diverted some to irrigate a patch of corn below our barn.

By August of the second summer, everything but that little irrigated patch had turned to tinder and the broom sage pastures at Silver Hill crinkled as you walked or rode through them. The quail moved into the bottoms next to the two little creeks. The incessant calling of the bobwhite was reduced to the one covey behind our barn. People were on edge, short with each other. There was a suspense to life, a waiting. I felt it, young as I was. We all knew the facts: we needed rain. Something had to give. And on August 16 of the second year, it did.

THE COUSINS OF THE professor had moved back to town from the summerhouses. They had decided that the heat would be more bearable in town than on the hill beneath the oaks with the breeze, because day after day the breeze was over ninety degrees. Finally they had had enough, and were gone. So they weren't to blame.

The sixteenth was a Saturday. I was still asleep when Matthew came to the kitchen door and hollered for my father. Our house was built on the side of the hill with the kitchen below and the bedrooms upstairs, and we were all still in bed. I knew Matthew's voice in all its tones. I had never heard him sound like he did that morning. It was fear that I heard. And before my father had pulled on his pants, I was on the side porch in my underwear, hollering down, "What's wrong? What's wrong?"

But I already knew. I could smell the smoke. I don't know why I hadn't smelled it in my little back bedroom under the bank unless the bank and the hill behind somehow diverted it. I was angry that I hadn't smelled it, that I had missed something so important.

"Where's your daddy, Charlie?" he hollered from below. "I need your daddy right now!" My father came to the porch, pulling on his old uniform khakis left over from the war and tucking in the khaki shirt. Gretchen was standing behind him in the doorway keeping her housecoat together with one hand while pulling her heavy hair away from her face with the other, still sleepy.

"Wait a minute, Matthew, I smell it!" he yelled and ducked back into the bedroom for shoes. By that time I had gotten into a pair of blue jeans and an undershirt and was therefore ready for a normal summer day.

"Charlie Lewis, you get back in that house and put on some shoes, right now. You hear me? This here's fire, and you ain't going to no fire barefoot." I glanced at my parents. No one was surprised that Matthew had said it first. It often fell to him to keep me in line, even though I was white and he was colored and it was almost the fifties. But our world was different— older and newer than the rest of the world back then.

Gretchen looked as if she might not let me go at all. But I dashed to my room and pulled out some school shoes, put them on without socks and tied them. By the time she was really awake and ready to intervene, the three of us were at Matthew's truck. I jumped into the middle, ready from habit to shift the floor shift as I often did when there were three of us. But Matthew was in a hurry and snatched the lever down into first and then to second before I was organized to help. No one said a word to start with, and by the time we got to the cattle guard above the lake no words were needed.

Because there it was. Just on the other side of the head of the lake, five hundred yards away from us. It was like being in church, but here you could see it. The fire looked alive and the noise was like a living thing speaking in tongues about its hunger and need for movement. The fire line was about a quarter of a mile wide, in a mature stand of field pines. A gentle southwest breeze was easing it steadily toward us and the fifty-acre broom sage field with the five-acre hog lot in the middle—with seven sows and a boar in it that summer. The summerhouses were to the north-northeast at the top of the hill, to our right, and the Corn House was straight ahead of the fire to the northeast over one hill behind where we were standing. Silver Hill was off to the east on the hill above the Corn House.

"What you think, Mr. Lewis? Better get Miz Lewis up to the big house. Something got to give here. Corn House. Big house. Summerhouses. At least one going to go. Maybe all of 'em. And the hogs. We going to lose them sure." He was almost breathless.

Then silence. Nothing but the fire and my father looking at it from under his dark brows. Then he slowly turned to Matthew and spoke in a voice entirely new to me. Slow, deliberate, and sure. Like a person walking a hazardous path for the twentieth time. Dangerous but sure.

"Go get Gretchen, Matthew. Take her to the big house. Then go to the village and get everyone you see and tell them all to go home and get a hard rake and a shovel. Tell them to leave their trucks behind the big house and come on foot from there. No use burning up half the trucks in the village if this thing gets away from us. Is Leonard's team in the pasture behind the big house? Get him to hook to the plow and come on. Ask Mr. Dudley to call the forestry people. They could bring a truckload of shovels and rakes, if nothing else." There was a pause. "That's it . . . No. Bring a couple of bucksaws, too."

He sounded like he was reading from a list, doing a daily procedure—my father who was always away on business during the week and was an outlander, my shy father who was often unsure around the people of the village. There was a small smile on his dark face.

Matthew took off.

"Is there a gap in this end of the hog lot, Charlie?"

"Yes sir, but it's hard to get open."

"Let's go."

We trotted down the hill. In a hurry, but not rushing. We got it open.

"Don't we have to run the hogs out, Daddy?"

"No, when that fire gets closer, the hogs will come out of there on their own. They'll be all right. But God knows where they'll end up. Matthew will know what to do about them."

At the summerhouse lane we stopped. He looked up and down figuring, talking his plan out loud. The lane was where he would try to stop the fire, using the lane as a break, but there were problems. The locust and cedar trees along the lane might catch and let the fire jump across. It all depended on how fast he got help and what the wind did. Of course, at the time I couldn't tell if he was talking to *me*. All I knew was that the fire had transformed my father into someone new to me. To a little kid, he was like a wizard peering out from under his brows, sometimes shading his eyes with his hand and squinting to get a better view, looking into the distance, although the fire was only five hundred yards away.

The breeze had all but stopped. The fire died down because now it had to move without the wind. It still looked alive, but resting, preparing for the future. It was waiting for something. It was waiting for the wind.

The professor arrived, out of breath. He looked at my father and saw the change in him and said, "Is there anything I can do, Charles? Gretchen is with us. I wouldn't be much help here what with my asthma . . . You know my family has lived in that house for 126 years. I would hate to lose it." Looking up at my father with a wistful smile on his seventy-year-old features, he said, "I know you will do everything you can."

"Of course, Professor. You know I will. It depends on the wind. We'll keep you posted."

His tone sounded military. But there had been no forest fires on the ships where he had been, in the Pacific, at Okinawa.

THE QUESTIONS ARISE: Why was he in charge? What qualified him? The answer certainly was not apparent that day. Much later, years later, he told me the story.

I was taking him to a consulting internist, and as we walked the halls of the hospital to the doctor's office, slowly, I heard myself saying, "Hurry up, Daddy, we'll be late." Then looking at his movement from the corner of my eye, I abruptly realized that he couldn't hurry up, that his time of hurry was over, that he would die, very soon. I knew this even before the internist took me aside, after examining him, and told me that his heart had grown big as a football and the time had come and I realized I still didn't know him.

LATER IN THE HOSPITAL, I asked—demanded, in a way, "Tell me about the beach at Okinawa. When you got the medal." I knew only the outline from the citation that I had read many times. He'd been the deck officer on the 150-foot gunboat—a ship so humble that it had no name, just a number—off the port side of another gunboat, both on radar picket duty, when a kamikaze struck the first one just behind the conning tower. It blew the side out of her. She was a goner.

Now I got the details. My father had brought his

ship alongside her, got all the pumps going, tied his ship to her at the risk of everything if they didn't get the fire out quick. It was the fire that almost got them all, with another kamikaze coming in. Both ships were loaded with ammunition. The way he described the chaos, I could see it: every gun on both ships blazing away at the kamikaze while the men fought the fire, and the pumps kept the crippled ship afloat—maybe both ships because he had tied them together. Daddy would have been on the conning tower, facing the suicide plane, firing away with his .45, surely the ultimate gesture of futility. But the big guns hit the plane good and, at the last minute, it swerved off to the side and went down clear of them. And then everyone on both ships was cheering and the fire was finally put out. That night, when they had backed out of the little bay, he and his men cut a steel plate from the deck of the injured ship and welded it into the hole in her side, against all the rules—"They could have court-martialed me for altering the hull of a ship without permission." But the ship went back on duty the next day, and they gave him a medal instead. I have kept the faded picture of him standing on the after deck of the ship, saluting.

He lasted only a week after he told me all this.

MATTHEW DROVE UP, his pickup encased in dust. He had Robert Paine with him. Robert used to look at me sideways, but he was always there when something big happened. Small and skinny under that deep black skin, he was full of enmity and humor. For once Robert was not smiling and didn't have a thing to say.

"What about Leonard? Is he coming?"

"Yes sir, he gone to get the team," replied Matthew. "He's harnessing up now. He'll be here."

Next, to my surprise, came the hunting Smiths — three truckloads of them. They drove right up to the cattle guard. There were seven in all. The grown-ups all looked alike — sallow, with wispy blond beards and tobacco juice stains. They were called the hunting Smiths because they lived off the countryside, although Lyman, the patriarch, owned seventy-five acres up the valley. The three boys each had a house, more like shacks, along the creek that ran through the farm. But it wasn't really a farm. Just some pasture and the rest woodland. They raised hogs and steers. But mainly they were hunters, year-round hunters. When I asked Matthew how they could hunt out of season he would change the subject, because in addition to the stock and the hunting, they made whiskey. They were the last of the whiskey makers. Some accommodation had been made. I never knew what. I had always been told to stay away from them. They would come to the village with their wives and half-dressed, dirty kids in the trucks, but they never stood around the potbelly to talk. The women would shop and return to the trucks while the men went across the road to the Texaco station to talk. I seldom went there. It was too dark. And the man who ran the station looked at me funny. The Smiths kept apart from us and we from them.

But there they were: the old man, the three sons, and their sons, who were about my age. They had rakes and shovels. One had a bucksaw. They were ready to go. They arrived just as my father finished up with the professor. Lyman, the old man, spoke. "We're here to do what we can, Mr. Lewis. Where do you reckon you'll try to stop her? At the lane here?"

My father nodded. "Could two of you ride the bed of one of the trucks up the outside of the lane and cut off the main branches of the trees hanging over the field? . . . But then don't you want to move your trucks back to Silver Hill? The wind might shift."

"Naw sir, I reckon we'll keep them near. Might need to get out of here in a hurry."

Everyone turned to. Within an hour there were twenty-three men. Leonard plowed a ditch the width of the plow ten feet in from the road and then another one ten feet in from the first. The two huge mares were panting like sheep as they finished. Normally Leonard let them rest at regular intervals. But not today. The men raked and shoveled the ground bare until they had a firebreak, using the two plowed ditches. The branches that hung over the break were cut back. This was done from the cattle guard to the summerhouses, a distance of almost a half mile. It was ten o'clock.

• • •

THE FIRE AND THE WIND had waited for us. The fire crept closer, but with very little breeze, it kept to just a creep. Because of the light wind, my father had been tempted in the beginning to fight the fire right at the edge of the existing fire line. But he decided there was too much danger. All that was needed was a few puffs of air before the firebreak was complete, and the fire would be past us. So he kept to his plan.

We waited. At ten-thirty it began. The breeze freshened from the southwest and the fire advanced into the field, leaving the burnt-out pines behind, moving closer to the hog lot. Suddenly a burst of wind drove the fire to the cedar-lined fence and the whole thing went up with a roar. I felt sick at my stomach, thinking of the hogs. But just after the cedars went up— even above the fire noise—we heard them squealing in terror and the whole group shot from the gap Daddy and I had opened in the pen.

Everyone laughed. As they came up the hill toward us, we yelled that those were the fastest hogs in history. It looked like they were coming right to us, but at the last moment they veered off toward the cattle guard, went streaming over—luckily no hog legs went through—and headed for Silver Hill. I looked back at the hog lot in time to see it go up in something almost like an explosion. Then it was gone. And all that was left were naked trees and the old barbed-wire fence hanging from its virtually fireproof posts. The place looked like the skeleton of a fish on a beach. The ground was covered with ash until a moment later the little spring in the center broke through, making a dark ribbon in the white ash as it made its way to the lake, as it always had.

The wind backed a little more to the south and picked up. What was going to happen next became stunningly apparent. We were going to lose the summerhouses. The fire would bypass our break. And we would watch, helpless as it roared north through the field toward the high oak woods surrounding the little compound of cabins with the big wooden water tank standing on its tower in the middle.

It was like a military campaign. My father moved his troops to his next line of defense in the big field behind our barn on the other side of the summerhouses. When the fire struck, it was like a mighty wind sucking the woods up into itself, making them disappear, eating up the cabins. And then, with a crash heard all the way at the village, the water tank went down, sending up a huge cloud of steam, momentarily dousing the fire in the compound before it went on, slowly now, toward the village itself.

Matthew was standing next to us when the fire left the woods. "She going to miss the Corn House, ain't she, Mr. Lewis? Wind done changed around some more. The village next, ain't it?"

My father nodded in an abstract way.

Then he hollered, "Lyman! Lyman!"

Lyman, who was twenty yards away, turned, stopped

chewing for a second, and looked at my father—speculation written on his sallow face with its wispy beard. Then he spat and started toward us. Lyman wasn't used to coming when someone called. It wasn't his nature. You could see what must have happened or at least something like it—when one time his old man had called him to him and then whipped his ass good for some misdemeanor, and Lyman swore somewhere inside himself never again to get in the position of having to come when someone called and by guile and just plain brains never having to.

But there was need here, no doubt. And Mr. Lewis had a look on his face like a man who knew what he was doing, what with his khakis like a uniform and his face streaked with soot, and all. So he came—even against his inclinations.

"Yes sir?"

"We've got to set a backfire at the village end of this ridge, on this side of the creek. Ten feet in. But we have to wait until the main fire comes off the bluff. If we set it too soon, it might jump the creek and burn down the village anyway. So you see? We have to wait. Get ourselves all lined up along the creek, ready to go. Your trucks are close. Can you and your boys go to the village and buy six or seven five-gallon cans and fill them with kerosene? Come back to the bridge at Holly House and we'll meet you there. Then we can spread out and lay the kerosene lines. We only have to go as far as the tracks. The fire won't jump the tracks.

Don't worry about the money for the cans and the kerosene. We'll settle up later. If we don't stop this fire, it won't make a lot of difference . . . God knows."

During this speech he stood with his hands on his hips, relaxed, with just a hint in his voice of the urgency he must have felt. Lyman smiled.

"I reckon we can do that. We going to have to set a line about six hundred yards, ain't we? We better get going. I ain't never seen a backfire, but I heard of one. Now I'm going to see one." He was still smiling as he called for his boys and they trotted off toward their trucks.

My father rounded up the rest of the group, and we started down the ridge to the bridge where Lyman would meet us. It was almost three-quarters of a mile from where we were standing to the creek next to the village. The breeze had died down again, but it whispered straight out of the southwest, slowly moving the fire toward the village. If it had been a windy day, the show would have been over already.

The Smiths were five minutes behind us. They had the kerosene, six cans of it. There must have been thirty grime-streaked men standing around my father when he gave the orders. The gist of it was that the Smith boys would start at the bridge, pouring out a trail of kerosene until the first can was empty. That person would stay at that point and the next can would keep the trail going. And so on until the kerosene trail extended up the creek all the way to where it paralleled the railroad. When the time came and Daddy gave the signal, the person with the can would light a rag or handkerchief and walk back down the line, lighting the trail—but not too fast. The whole line must be lit. Then we would find out.

The rest of the men were spread out between the backfire line and the creek, in case they were needed to keep the backfire from burning too close to the creek, which was only fifteen feet wide, bank to bank. Matthew and I stayed at the bridge at the upper end of the line.

The fire whispered its way toward us. Everyone was lined up. The kerosene trails were down. We waited. My father was halfway up the line, on the side of the little hill where everyone could see him. He was standing with his hands on his hips again, glancing from the fire to the men, with only a T-shirt on now, the khaki shirt torn up to make the torches for the kerosene. I stood close to Matthew. I could feel my gut drawing up, could hear Matthew's breathing change as the breeze picked up and the fire hesitated before its final plunge down the hill toward us, and the village. Half the people of the village were on the other side of the creek watching. No one said a word.

Then Daddy let out a yell and the Smith boys started down their lines. The tinder broom sage flashed up as if fueled by gasoline, not just kerosene. In an instant the backfire took on a life of its own.

Burning high off the ground, spreading both ways—toward the creek and toward the oncoming main fire. We wondered if it would spread to the creek before it merged with the big fire. The breeze picked up again and the big fire roared down the slope.

Matthew and I watched from our end of the line. When the two fires were twenty-five feet apart, the backfire, sucked up into a maelstrom, stopped advancing toward the creek and leaped back into the arms of the big fire. It was an explosion when they came together. The roar became deafening. Everyone crouched to the ground, almost in terror. The fireball left the ground, having run out of fuel.

And that was all. There was quiet. The fire had eaten itself.

Then the cheering started, Daddy and Lyman laughing and shaking hands—the stranger and the native. People came streaming across the creek, women shouting at their men. Kids running to fathers. People stared at the blackened ground where only a few minutes ago the fire had threatened their livelihoods if not their lives, where now there was nothing.

For me what remained was my father, standing alone in the little piece of blackened bottom land, with his smile. It was as if I had never seen him before, a stranger come into our midst in time of need, a stranger who would probably leave as suddenly as he had come.

Gretchen was running from the road and then so

was I. The three of us embraced and there were tears from Gretchen and from me, too.

But even then, the voice in the back of my mind kept asking who he was and where he would go when he left, when Monday came, and he was gone again, on business.

Winter Run

THE LAND WAS OLD and acid and used only for grazing and garden plots. Because it hardly ever snowed in
that part of Virginia, the color of winter there was
more often reddish brown than white. The fence lines
had grown up in multiflora rose and cedars, and broom
sage had become the main grass. The farming wasn't
much unless you were rich, but the hunting was good.
During the war the deer had begun to come back, and
now there was venison for special days. It was a time
between times, although we didn't know it.

In 1950 the winter began in earnest in December
and was so different and so bad that it was known for
years after as the Great Winter. No one died—but a
fuel-oil truck slid across a lane down the bank into the
creek and stayed there for two months before they

could get it out. Deep paths had to be opened up through the snow so the cows could get to water. And if you came from the cold into a barn insulated and made silent by snow, you made a sudden passage into a world so warm and secure you might remember it for the rest of your life.

Between storms Leonard Waits, who was a black man with nearly white skin, plowed out all the lanes in the neighborhood. His team of tall gray workhorse mares named Jewel and Queen were so strong they could pull the old wooden snow plow through the drifts so cars and trucks could get out.

Leonard also owned old Bat, of course. Most people thought she was at least twenty-five, although Leonard swore she was thirty-five, and worthless. But that was just his excuse for leaving her all winter at Silver Hill, because every spring he came and got her to plow all the gardens in the neighborhood, and charged people for it.

Old Bat's brown body had begun to sag away from her absolutely straight backbone like a mountain shack whose ridge pole, against all odds, stays level as the shack falls in around it. But she was still spry, as you know, and liked to escape from her pasture and go on rambles around the neighborhood. Strangers had been known to rush into the store in the village to report an escaped mule only to be greeted with a bored and cursory nod.

When she wanted to go somewhere, she walked up to the fence, cocked her head to get the distance, lowered her hind end, raised her front end, and hopped over—even if the fence was five feet high. She was best known for her bray. It began with the usual mule whistle, but the second part was spectacular and sounded something like a tenor tugboat. In spite of being an extra animal to feed, her braying made her welcome at Silver Hill each winter because Professor James said that Bat's braying reminded him of the first cavalry charge at the second battle of Manassas. When Bat brayed at night, Gretchen, reflecting her raising as a strict Catholic, thought the old mule sounded like the end of the world.

Silver Hill was at the top of the hill, the home place in the center of a six-hundred-acre farm, which was almost all pasture. We lived at the foot of the hill in the house my father had converted from a corncrib and rented from Professor James.

My bonding with the land came about because Matthew Tanner was close at hand and willing to take on an impatient white kid as a disciple. I spent all the time I could with Matthew. I was a nuisance, but it was his nature to be giving, so he put up with my endless questions about the land and wildlife. He only sent me home once—when I set a pile of leaves on fire before he was ready.

Matthew and Sally lived in a cottage behind the house at Silver Hill. Matthew took care of the little home farm and the gardens. Sally took care of the big house. She churned her own butter and rolled it with wooden paddles into those little round balls like you think you'd get at Buckingham Palace. But she didn't like kids.

After each storm that winter, walks to the village became adventures. There were the tracks of possums and raccoons and foxes. Sometimes I saw the animals themselves making their way down the plowed road rather than floundering around in the deep snow of the fields. Nearly every day, deer stood in the lee of a huge rock up the hill from the creek that paralleled the lane. When they saw me, they leapt up the hillside on their springy legs and disappeared in a spray of snow.

Then the dogs came into our lives—apparently from nowhere. I was enormously pleased whenever I saw them on the road. There was the tingle of danger about them. Even though I always whistled and called out, they looked at me and ran, with their tails tucked and their heads raised like wild animals. There were four of them. Nothing had been done about them because the snow was so deep. It was hard enough just to get the chores done, let alone trying to kill wild dogs that disappeared whenever you looked for them.

When the first thaw set in and it was easier to get around, the dogs killed two grown sheep at the Joneses in broad daylight while the family was in the village shopping. A few days after the sheep were killed, I heard the dogs barking on the run over the ridge behind the rock. It wasn't the long, drawn-out note of the coonhounds; this sound was sharp and hoarse and staccato. I could see Bat on the other hill, with her big ears cocked, listening to them also. In the mist rising from the thaw, she looked all gray and weathered, like a ghost watching over the land.

The first dog, a tan longhaired bitch, came down the ridge, mute, and crouched beneath the overhang of the rock. Then a doe came into sight, panting and weaving from side to side, her tongue hanging out— exhausted. The three dogs behind her were trotting, but still a little cautious. The tan bitch shot out from beside the rock and grabbed the doe by the tongue as she went by, slamming into her sideways. Down they went and the other three piled on top. The doe let out a long bleat as the dogs growled and struggled with her.

I crossed the creek on a game trail and edged my way up the bank for a closer look. When the tan bitch raised her head and saw me, unlike most animals, she locked her yellow eyes onto mine for a second. Then she rose up a little, pulled back her lips, and snarled from down low in her chest. She scared the hell out of me, for a fact. I jumped back across the creek and ran down the lane and up the hill to Silver Hill, looking for Matthew.

He was milking. When I ran into the little barn and smelled the cow and heard her chewing and the milk swishing in the bucket, I came to my senses and blurted out what had happened. Matthew sat on the little stool, his hands on the cow's teats. As I told the story, he gripped the teats harder and harder until the cow flinched. That was all he showed, sitting there in his own quietness, his leather baseball cap pushed back from his broad forehead.

When he finished milking, we got into the pickup and drove down to our lane with the single-barrel 12-gauge resting on the seat and floorboards between us.

"We've got to kill them!" I said. "Just like they killed the doe—don't we?"

"We'll see," he said. "Ain't much chance we can get around downwind without them seeing us. And, anyway, the son-of-a-bitches probably won't stay. Just kill and go after eating a little gut." It was the first time I'd ever seen him really angry or heard him use bad language.

At the turn, he stopped the truck. We crossed the creeks and eased our way along in the shelter of the bank until we were close to the rock. Suddenly, he jumped up the bank, pulled back the hammer, and fired at the tan bitch before I realized that the dogs were still there, growling and tugging at the carcass. He hit her—knocked her down for a second—but she didn't squeal like you would have thought a dog would. All she did was let out a sharp little bark, and all four were gone before he could reload.

We stood there for a moment, silent, staring at the ripped open doe. Then he said, "C'mon, Charlie, we got to skin out this deer, and I need you to help me."

When we were finished, we loaded up the carcass and the hide and drove the half mile to the village and pulled into the parking lot, with the dirty snow piled all around. The potbelly in the store was glowing and people were talking before they went home. Matthew told the story of me and the doe, while everyone nodded approval.

Then Fred Henry spoke up. "It's the snow what done it, Matthew. What with not being able to get around the farm much less go hunting. But now it's eased up, and we got to kill 'em. You know about the sheep. Now listen to what happened to me night before last." Fred became declamatory.

"Well, there I was, sitting, looking out the window, listening to the radio, and the moon full, and me just looking into the moonlight. And all of a sudden the cow in my back pasture throwed up her head and took off with her calf just flying and me wondering what the devil's going on.

"Then I seen the dogs. They come across from my back fence. I got the gun and headed for the pasture. But when that tan bitch seen me, she give out with that little bark you talked about and the whole bunch throwed up their heads and were gone. But they come back in the night, because the next morning that calf was laying dead in the middle of a patch of churned up snow.

"They may be just dogs, but they've sure God gone bad, and we got to kill 'em, Matthew. I ain't never in my life seen anything like that tan bitch. She looks at you like she knows more than you do. And now that they can bring down a wild doe, running in a pack, Lord knows what will be next. Trouble is they ain't scared like they was wild. They just come and kill."

When Fred had finished, Matthew turned to Fred's brother, Luke, who was the older of the brothers and was section foreman on the C & O Railroad. He was tall and looked like a black Paul Bunyan. He wore hunting boots with his trousers tucked in and a stocking cap and a mackinaw. The brothers dressed the same and looked the same, except Fred talked and was short. Luke was quiet and he kept hounds, hounds that would run anything you put them onto.

"Do you reckon it's eased up enough to bring the hounds in the morning, Luke?" Matthew asked. "I know where they're laying up."

This revelation turned heads, mine included.

Luke nodded and Matthew continued, "I'll get Leonard and Robert. You and Fred bring the hounds. The old summerhouse foundations is where they're staying when they ain't hunting. I seen them the other night and tracked them in the snow. You and Fred can walk in with the hounds, and we'll be at the three crossings; and if you jump them, at least one of us will get a shot most likely. The wind might be wrong, but we got to chance it. Maybe they'll run the country and not the wind."

Then he said to me, "Reckon your daddy would come, Charlie?"

I said I was sure he would, bursting with pride once again that my Pennsylvania-born father, the virtual foreigner in that land, would be asked to help. He had an out-of-character and uncanny ability with a .22, so when precision shooting with no side effects was required, he was asked. Like the time a bat bothered a lady at evening prayer and Daddy was commissioned to shoot it and not mess up the church. I remember him sitting in the front pew on the Epistle side, dressed in a Sunday suit, waiting while the bat flew around and finally landed under the eave on the dark pine plate. I remember him bringing up the rifle real slow and hitching his body around to make the shot less awkward, hearing his breath ease out, the little crack from the short-short, and the bat falling dead. And I remember wanting to cheer, but being afraid to because we were in church. Yes, I was sure he would come.

Matthew took me home. My father came to the door and stood there kind of skinny and awkward with the backlight making shadows across his hawk nose and deep-set eyes. He agreed that something had to be done, particularly in the light of the doe being killed. He would be glad to come, and it would be fine to meet at the store at six.

It was a restless night—probably for my father, too. From the distance of years, I remember him as always completely cool, but it is an unlikely memory.

The next morning, they were waiting for us around a fire they had built next to the hog-scalding tub at the branch. The hounds were baying in excitement in the hound boxes on the pickups. Besides Luke and Fred and Leonard, there was Robert Paine. He drank some and had done time on the road gang and, as I've mentioned before whenever something big happened Robert was always there. And, of course, Matthew, who knew what to do even though he'd never seen such a winter or heard of a pack of wild dogs before. You could see in the firelight the tension etched into their shadowy faces. It had been a long winter.

Luke and Fred and the hounds headed for the burnt-out summerhouses above Silver Hill where the ridge that ran almost to the village began. Robert and Leonard went to the crossing behind the barn at our house. They put my father halfway down the ridge, above where I had seen the doe killed. Matthew and I would be at the end closest to the village. Matthew had Professor James's old double-barrel 16-gauge. We crossed the creek and stood next to the rock outcropping at the end of the ridge. We couldn't actually see my father's stand, but sound carried well so we would know what was happening if they came our way. There was a rock pile at the other end of the ridge, across the lane from where the summerhouses had been, and that was where the dogs were spending the nights. Luke said later that before the hounds were a hundred yards from the rocks, they put their noses to the ground and began waving their tails, showing that they had caught the scent of the dogs' night lines. They could see the bloody tracks of the bitch in what was left of the snow. When the hounds started whining and pulling at the leads, the men turned them loose. Almost at once they burst into full cry. Those dogs may have just been dogs, but they sure smelled wild. Luke and Fred looked up to see the quarry crossing the lane in a tight bunch, heading south, up the wind, straight away from us. Two things saved the situation. The first was that they were heading for unfamiliar territory. And the second was old Bat. The dogs had veered a little to the east, and just as it looked like the show was over, or would never start, there came a bellow so loud that Matthew and I heard it at the other end of the ridge. There is nothing on earth that sounds as disgruntled as a pissed-off mule. And old Bat was really pissed.

Having escaped for whatever reason, Bat had decided to go a new way and had ambled down the lane toward the lake where the pipe cattle guard was across it so trucks could cross but cows couldn't. When she got to the cattle guard, she walked right into the thing up to her knees and hocks and was stuck. Being a sensible mule, she didn't struggle, she bellowed. And that turned the dogs back to the northeast, heading down wind, toward us.

So with old Bat bellowing and the black and tans throwing their tongues like the end of the world as the hunt became a sight chase, my stomach jerked up into a knot that grew even tighter when we heard shots. Leonard and then Robert had let go with their single-barrel 12-gauges and killed the first two. In spite of the shots, the last two kept running hard downwind rather than risk making the turn back into unfamiliar country. So they went right past my father. The crack of the .22 long rifle hollow point sounded and another one went down.

This left the last one for Matthew and me, and him

with the double barrel. It was the tan bitch. As she rounded the end of the ridge with the hounds in hot pursuit and the winter funneling down to that moment, she looked back and hesitated as if to make sure the whole thing was for real and not just a game and maybe we could go home now. Matthew fired once and this time she didn't get up.

As I held on to the sleeve of his old denim coat, trying not to cry and looking back and forth from the bitch to Matthew, I could feel the tension so hot in him I thought for a second he might shoot her again. But as we stood there watching the light go out of her eyes and the blood spreading around her like a snow cone, I felt him ease and saw his eyes change and soften. And when I looked again she was dead.

The wind had stopped and beneath the leaden winter sky the voice of a single crow filled the echoed silence of the morning. The hounds went over to smell the bitch's body, to be sure of what it was they had been running. When the others came up, there wasn't much to be said—running dogs with hounds had a bad feel to it, but at least now they were gone.

All that was left to do was free old Bat. Matthew and I agreed to meet up at the cattle guard just as soon as he finished milking. We figured she could last that long because it was not her nature to struggle, and she had gotten tired of bellowing. The rescue turned out to be quite a job. What happened was that after the affront of our not coming to get her immediately, when we finally did arrive to save her, she wouldn't budge. It was one of those soft winter, late mornings with the clouds low and smooth when sound carries and there is no wind and the temperature is about fifty degrees. The hillside was like an auditorium with wonderful acoustics and Matthew and Bat and me as the characters in some comic farce.

First we pried up two pipes and tried to get her to step out front end first and then the back end. The mule, however, was not interested. She had developed the ability to concentrate all the weight of her nearly thousand-pound bulk in one leg at a time so that not even Matthew's inordinate strength could budge her. So back to the pry bar we went, and while we were heaving at the next pipe nearest her hindquarters, she turned her huge old head around until her sighted eye was aimed at us. And as if that was not enough to supervise the operation properly, she cocked one ear around to be sure she was taking everything in.

As we pried with the bar, I began to see the morning's hunt over and over, and then the scene at the rock when the dogs had killed the doe. And although I am probably imagining it, I seem to remember that the day grew a little colder and the clouds a little closer. And I was glad when Bat finally stepped out of the cattle guard, and we could lead her home and I could walk down the hill to the Corn House and Gretchen's grilled cheese sandwiches.

That should have been the end of it. But no one would let it alone. After all the versions of the great dog hunt had been told, and everyone had laughed at Bat's antics, we still didn't know where the dogs had come from or how they had lived before they started killing livestock. Or how they had learned to run down wild deer, being just farm dogs. The questions lingered like the dirty snow from the winter the likes of which we had never seen before either.

SPRING CAME. Things worked back toward normal. Leonard went around the neighborhood plowing gardens with Bat and, to my disgust, I was back at school. One day when Leonard wasn't using her, Bat, who was still living at Silver Hill, went for a ramble up the summerhouse lane. My mother saw her going and called the Jameses. Sally, who had the same opinion of Bat as she had of me, reluctantly agreed to find Matthew. Later that morning, he walked up the lane and brought the old mule back.

When I got home from school that day, I went to find Matthew and see if anything was happening. "C'mon, Charlie, let's walk up the summerhouse lane. I got something to show you." Bat was out for the second time that day and we let her come ambling along behind us.

Halfway up, the lane cut through a bulge in the land, leaving four-foot banks on either side. A dismembered deer carcass lay there, skewed and weathered. You could see tooth marks on the long bones.

We stood silent for a moment, looking at it, with

me holding on to Matthew's sleeve again with old Bat right behind us, ears cocked.

"Leonard found a carcass like this over at Joe Stephens's farm last week. Do you see what happened, Charlie?" he asked.

But I didn't, not at first.

"There was a drift here between the banks," he said. "They run her up the lane, and when she hit the deep snow, she went down, and they caught her. Just like us, that doe didn't know nothing about no winter and deep snow. I don't reckon we'll ever find out where they come from, but that's how they learned to run down a deer. It was the snow what taught 'em."

And suddenly I could see it in my mind's eye: the tan bitch waiting at the foot of the lane, taking up the chase as the deer went by; and the other three, winded, beginning to flag; and her barking the sight chase, the deer running hard; and the final surge as the deer hit the drift and went down; the bitch reaching for the throat hold and the other three piling on.

And then again, the hounds in full cry and Matthew with the double barrel, waiting, as the bitch rounded the little bluff and looked back—to be sure it wasn't just a game.

The Mule Dies

SHE WAS VERY OLD. Despite Leonard Waits's insistence that she was thirty-five, most of us agreed that she was in her twenty-fifth year, and no one had ever heard of a mule living to that age before. She had long been a figure of importance. Not only was she the last mule in the area, she was a mule of independent and eccentric mind. As mentioned, even at her advanced age, she refused to stay in a pasture when she got the notion to ramble around. And even though she lived on the professor's charity, she and Leonard still plowed all the gardens in the neighborhood every spring.

Her blind eye had long ago turned a milky white. As a result, she had a strange way of cocking her head around to get her sighted eye on what she was looking at. She had a curious habit of standing on a hilltop, staring out over the land, unmoving, like an ancient stone marker. Professor James said she was like something you might read about in the Old Testament. But we always took the professor with a grain of salt. After all, *he* was so eccentric he once told Matthew that he liked the smell of skunk because it made his asthma feel better.

Bat had been among us for so long that people who were grown and had families could remember giving her an apple or a carrot when they were kids.

The previous winter, when the four domestic dogs gone wild had killed a doe right in front of Charlie as he was walking in the lane from the store, Charlie'd had the hell scared out of him. We all had.

Our little village had been snowed in to the point that school had not kept since Thanksgiving and the drifts had piled up ten feet deep in some places. It wasn't supposed to snow like that in Virginia. We were barely able to do the chores and be sure the cows had paths to get to water. Then came the dogs. It was like an old tale about wolves. But Charlie would tell you at the drop of a hat, and at the top of his voice, that it was no fairy tale that afternoon when he saw the dogs drive the doe up to the rock where the tan bitch was waiting. Certainly no tale when she pulled the doe down by her tongue and the rest piled on and killed her. After that, some families wouldn't let their children walk to the store alone. It wasn't until the January thaw that we could deal with the dogs. Matthew Tanner organized the hunt with Luke Henry's hounds.

Bat had gotten stuck in the cattle guard just as the hunt got under way. The result was her spectacular bellow of fury.

And so at that late date in her long life she became a hero and the subject of tales told in the evening around the potbelly in the store. And much laughter. Who had ever heard of a mule saving a hunt for wild dogs? And Charlie's eyes would squint as he listened to the tone of the laughter, until he was sure no one was making fun of her.

THAT SPRING SHE began to fail. Leonard Waits came for her and tried to plow gardens as usual, but she was so slow he got impatient and used Queen, one of his giant workhorse mares. Queen was too big for the job, but what was he to do?

So Bat spent her days on the edge of the garden patch, with the creek right there for water and shade under the paradise trees. Charlie gave her last year's hay from the barn and fed her by hand with grass cut with a sickle. At the time of Bat's death, Charlie's father was in Philadelphia during the week because he had a job with a company that would be moving to Virginia to get away from labor unions.

Charlie's mother, whose people were from Sweden, was tall and had a slender figure. She was what you might call willowy—a cool beauty. She was in her early thirties. She loved to garden, but she didn't like

the animals much. Some of us felt she was too moth-
erly with Charlie. And Charlie, at eleven, was in full
rebellion against it.

THE WEEK BEFORE Bat died, she took a walk
up to the big house. Professor James, who taught law
at the university in town and was famous, was preparing a speech he was to give in New York City the next
week. The professor had lived among us all his life,
and his family from time almost out of mind. We
weren't exactly sure what made him famous, but anyone who went to New York City to give speeches was
not your everyday person. Also, when a family was
in need, help would come, anonymously, through the
post office. The professor would receive a letter of
thanks and smile and say it must be a mistake, but it
was nice that there were people who would help out in
hard times.

As the professor watched from his study window,
the old mule made her way up the lane. He said later
that there was no doubt in his mind that she was nearing the end, but that she also seemed so old as to
be somehow beyond death—in his fancy phrase, "a
fleshly rendering of something mythic." The professor,
who was tall and thin and old and who, some of us
felt, bore a gaunt resemblance to Bat himself, was
concerned about her that morning. And being unable
to find Matthew, he called the Corn House and got
Charlie who said he would be right up to get her.

The two of them stood on the porch watching as

Bat, who had stopped her ramble, nibbled some grass on the edge of the lane.

"Will she die, Professor?"

"Why, yes," he replied, "she surely will die, as must we all, Charlie. You know that."

"But not soon," Charlie said. It was a statement.

"She looks pretty feeble, don't you think, Charlie?"

"Yes sir, but why does she have to die now? I don't want her to die!"

"She has had a long life and, in terms of the usual mule life, I would have to think a good one. And of course she is a hero. Yes, she can certainly die now without reproach. All things pass in their time. You must remember that Charlie . . . Now you take her back down the hill. We don't want her to get too tired out, do we?"

"No sir, I guess not. It's just—"

"You run along with her, Charlie. I'm busy working on my speech."

But the professor said later that he had sent Charlie along with Bat because he was afraid the boy was about to cry. After all, he was still only eleven. And the professor wasn't sure about how to handle tears in an eleven-year-old, having never had any children of his own.

So back down the hill they went, Charlie leading Bat and talking to her in his strident voice. The professor could hear him all the way back up at the big house. But he couldn't make out the words.

• • •

CHARLIE WAS AS MUCH a character in the neighborhood as Bat though he looked like any other eleven-year-old of the time. He had a crew cut and was skinny and his nose, inherited from his father, was big. So it was not so much what he looked like as what he did and said that caused his fame. He talked in a voice that was loud and grating and carried far.

Each June when school let out, the first thing Charlie did was take off his shoes and declare that he was not going to put them back on until September. When Charlie first took this notion, he said he wasn't going to wear shoes all summer, period. But his mother rose up in arms over that and stated that she was not going to have Charlie seen in church without shoes. It would look as if the Lewis family couldn't afford to buy shoes for their son. So a compromise was struck, and Charlie was allowed to go barefoot even to town as long as he agreed to wear his shoes to church.

His other habit had to do with reading. From the time he got to the fourth grade, he would, each summer—as with the shoes—publicly state that it was his intention to unlearn how to read. Not forever, just for the summer. Charlie was so serious about this that he refused to acknowledge he could read the labels on the merchandise in the store when his mother sent him for groceries. When asked about it, he would become shy, as if he himself didn't know exactly why he did it.

There was also, of course, the way Charlie was with Bat. It had started when he was a little boy. One day

Professor James saw Charlie walk up to Bat in the back pasture. She was standing in front of the old smokehouse, which was no longer used and was beginning to sag—although if the breeze was in your face it would still make your mouth water from all those hundreds of hams and shoulders that had been cured in there. Charlie was holding out some grass for old Bat to eat. There was plenty of grass for her without having to lift her head for a five-year-old. But the old mule raised up her head, cocked it around so she could see the little boy, and gently took the grass from his hand. Her head and ears were almost as tall as the whole boy. When the professor described this encounter, his eyes would go distant. He said it was the sweetest thing he'd ever seen.

From then on Charlie and Bat were close. She could hear him coming and would turn her head around to see him. Her huge ears would go forward as if she could somehow see through them, too. Bat was a pretty tame mule, but even so, most mules are a little bad about getting caught up from the pasture. But she would wait for Charlie. Then you would hear his grating voice, talking to her in regular language, not the fake baby talk people use to talk with animals. But no one ever quite got what he said because if you came close he would stop, as if embarrassed.

Charlie also spoke to grown-ups in a grown-up way. There was an urgency to what he said that often outweighed the message. If he wanted to go possum hunting, he would ask Luke Henry, who owned the hounds, when he was going next. Not in the tone of voice of request, but urgently. It wasn't impatience. It was something more somehow.

As Charlie grew older and started to school, Bat would sometimes go on a ramble that ended up at the school bus where Charlie got off. Some of us thought it happenstance. But if you heard Charlie say hello to her in that normal language, as he stepped from the bus, you might wonder. And if you saw him trudging in the upper lane with old Bat walking behind him, swinging her long ears in perfect step with the boy, or the two of them outlined in winter light against a leaden December sky, or stopping to look out over the fields side by side, you would know that it was not happenstance that brought them together.

AND SO THAT AFTERNOON Charlie returned Bat to the lot, cut her some fresh grass with the sickle, and went home.

One week later, when old Bat brayed at dawn, even Gretchen knew something was wrong. It was not Bat's usual bray. This one began with the bellow and ended with the whistle. The reverse of the usual. And the whistle was long and drawn out and gradually faded away.

By the time the whistle stopped, Charlie was out of bed and running, in his underpants—no time for clothes, let alone shoes—running across the garden plot with his already tough bare feet and his mind unencumbered by the knowledge of reading, knowing that she was dead.

But even then in the sudden, slow coil of his mind, he must have begun the shift from life to death, begun to make the connection between the dead doe and the dead dogs—and old Bat. And he must have heard again the professor's words: *All things pass in their time, Charlie.*

You can see Charlie bursting into tears of outrage, saying, *No!* to the dead mule lying before him, with her tongue hanging out and already beginning to go dry, and her milky eye looking up like a huge marble.

So just as he had done after he saw the dogs kill the doe, he started up the hill for Matthew, who had seen lots of dead things, including people, and would know what to do. Charlie found him milking, sitting on the little stool, his cap pushed back against the early summer heat. And just as before, when Charlie smelled the cow and heard the milk swishing in the bucket, he came to his senses and told his story. "She's dead!"

Then silence, except for the slow buzz of a wasp and the splashing of the milk and the chewing of the cow. Matthew gazed steadily at Charlie with his dark eyes—eyes that had turned bloodshot many years before, as if the accumulated burden of all they had seen had at some point suddenly burst the tiny vessels in the whites.

"She had to die, Charlie. That's what happens. You know that. She had to die."

Sobbing, almost unable to speak, Charlie said, "What are we going to do with her? We can't just leave her there." And again: "What will we do with her? . . . Not pull her over the hill to the boneyard. She's not a cow! She's old Bat!"

Then Matthew said softly, "Charlie, go home and get your breakfast. Soon as I finish milking, I'll call down to the store. Most likely Leonard will be there. In a while we'll figure out what to do."

At nine o'clock Matthew arrived with Leonard. Robert Paine was also with them. Robert had been on his way to sickle the honeysuckle off the bank below Mrs. White's garden next to the church when he heard the news from Matthew that old Bat had died and Charlie was going to be a problem. So Robert said to heck with the bank. He was going to see what that crazy white boy would do. They got out of the pickup, three black men dressed in bib overalls with leather baseball caps on, even though it was June, and blue work shirts. They stood next to the truck waiting for Charlie. When Charlie came out of the house they went down the lane to the garden patch, crossed the little irrigation ditch, and walked over to the mule. Her dry tongue was hanging farther out of her mouth, touching the ground, and a single fly buzzed around her head.

Leonard spoke first. "Well, Matthew, I reckon you need to carry me home so I can get the team and pull this dead mule back over the hill to the boneyard. She'll sure start to stink if she stays here. And I know

Miz Lewis don't want no stinking mule this close to her house."

Matthew pushed his cap back even farther. "I don't know," he said. "This was a right special mule. Don't you reckon we ought to bury her?"

"Do what?" barked Leonard. "Bury her? What you talking about bury her? I ain't digging no hole to bury that huge old mule in and her with only one eye to boot! Dig a hole, I reckon!"

Robert let out a snort. He said later that he knew this was going to be good, because although Matthew Tanner was a physically powerful man, not even he would have had any idea of burying that mule single-handed. And it was a mighty favor to ask two grown men, white or black, to help bury a mule that ought to be drug over the hill where she belonged and forgot about—just because some skinny white boy whose family didn't even own any land wanted him to.

"Professor James—," Matthew began, but Leonard interrupted.

"I ain't studying on no Professor James, Matthew. If he wants that mule buried, then let him come do it his self. I ain't doing it, period." Leonard would never have spoken to Professor James like that to his face, but Leonard was under the strain of an outrageous idea that looked like it might actually take hold and he was out of control.

After a period of silence, Matthew, with Charlie gripping his sleeve, shifted his stance, looked right at Leonard and Robert and said, "Professor James is in

New York City doing a speech, but he's taking the night train. He'll be home first thing in the morning. We'll just wait till then. She won't start to stink too bad before then . . . We'll just let it be for now."

Again, silence. There was staring back and forth, but no contest. Matthew stood still, quiet. People—black and white—respected Matthew. That is, they did what he said, and not just because he worked for Professor James.

When Matthew got back from taking the men to the store, Charlie was waiting, his face splotched from dried tears. He said, "Why don't we get Johnny Griggs's backhoe? You know that thing that dug the ditch at the Esso station. That thing could dig the hole in nothing flat, and then she'd be buried and wouldn't have to be drug up the lane and over the hill to the boneyard by her neck and the hair skinning off and all. Anyway, there hasn't been anything put in that place for years. Why should she?" Then he started to cry, clutching Matthew's sleeve as he always did in an emergency—standing in the early June heat: the almost frail, white boy and the black man on whom so many of us depended.

"Now Charlie, you listen here. She's dead and ain't nothing going to bring her back. She wouldn't know nothing about it if we was to drag her over the hill, she being dead . . ."

"But *we* would," Charlie choked out. "*We* would know about it. And it would be like her life hadn't meant anything if we don't bury her. It would be like we forgot what she did when she turned the wild dogs, and when she used to get out and stand on top of a hill watching things out of her one eye, and when she snatched that tomato right out of Miss Farnley's grocery sack and we all laughed. . . . If we don't bury her, it will be like she never lived." He stopped. He was out of breath. But the final recognition of the situation had set in. His mind had turned all the way around. And now it was time to do something. "What about the backhoe, Matthew?" he asked.

"The backhoe!" Matthew said. "Lord only knows what it would cost to get that machine out here to bury a dead mule. It don't make sense. Just wait. When I meet the professor at the train in the morning, I'll try to talk him into getting a gang together to dig the hole."

AFTER IT WAS ALL OVER, we realized that there was plenty of warning that Charlie was going to do something. No sooner had Matthew said he had to go to the co-op for dairy feed, Charlie went home and told his mother he was going to walk to the village. Charlie set out with shoes and a shirt on. Mr. Dudley, who was postmaster and owned the store, saw Charlie standing outside the post office door, reading the bus schedule posted on the wall, against his rule that he could not read in the summer.

Charlie walked over to the bus stop. The town was still small and the village smaller so it was not unusual for him to go to town by himself for a dentist appointment or the like. He was early for the next bus. Leonard's cousin, Frank Maupin, saw him standing at the stop and pulled over to ask if he wanted a ride to town. Charlie said yes, thank you, that would be nice.

The word of old Bat's death and the argument over her burial had gotten around. Frank said he was sorry that she had died, knowing how partial Charlie was to her. But she was dead now and Charlie should just let them drag her over the hill to the boneyard the way it always used to be done with dead stock.

"She's not dead stock," Charlie said in a tight voice. "She is Bat, the mule . . ." His voice trailed off uncharacteristically. Frank glanced over at Charlie; the boy appeared to him to be really pale and he looked as if he was gritting his teeth. Frank also noticed the shoes and the shirt.

"Where do you need to go in town, Charlie?"

"Could you drop me off at Eighth and Main, please?" Charlie replied. "I need to see Dr. Stokes for my shots."

Now Frank knew that Dr. Stokes's office was a good five blocks from Eighth and Main. But Charlie seemed so sure of himself, Frank just let him off without giving it any more thought.

Griggs Construction at that time owned a dump truck in which Johnny hauled his daddy's old Ford tractor with a scrape blade that he used to finish his excavating jobs. Behind the truck he pulled a trailer with the pride of his life on board: a brand new fifty-horsepower Allis-Chalmers tractor with a Woods backhoe on the back. It was the first and only one in the county. He had a track loader but it stayed parked in the yard behind the office much of the time now that he had the backhoe.

Johnny's family lived on a small farm that they had owned for three generations and from which they could not quite scratch a living. So in addition to farming, Johnny's father had worked at Hick's Silk Mill for most of his adult life to keep the family and the farm together.

Johnny had enlisted in the navy in '42 and because he was good with tractors he ended up in the Seabees building airfields on Pacific islands. When the war was over, he came home, borrowed five thousand dollars with his daddy's farm as collateral, bought the equipment, and proceeded to make a success of himself. Mainly he dug basements for the new houses springing up in the county as the university began to expand and businesses from the north moved in.

Then the first all-hydraulic backhoe attachments became available. This was the machine Johnny had wished for in the Pacific, but the war was over before they were ready for the market. Now, if he had a bigger tractor with the backhoe attached, he could expand his business. The bank lent him another five thousand. Johnny figured out what he had to get to make his payments and some profit—twenty-five dollars an hour. No one had ever heard of such a price for a single piece of machinery. Also, the backhoe was a whole new thing. Nobody was sure what it could do.

Johnny stayed busy with the other equipment, but business for the backhoe was slow, because drain fields were still dug by hand. He wasn't getting enough jobs to make the payments. He was worried.

But you would never have guessed it. He always wore khakis—pants and shirt—short sleeves in the summer, long sleeves in winter. He also wore aviator's dark glasses. He looked like a "can-do" man. He had smooth, tanned skin over heavy muscles, and a square, well-boned face.

"Well, hi Charlie," he said when Charlie stepped into his office. "What are you doing here? . . . Look at that, you have shoes on."

Charlie started right in with his usual urgency. "Johnny, I've got a job for the backhoe. Have you heard about old Bat? She died this morning, early. At the garden patch next to our house. We need to bury her. Professor James would want her buried, but he is in New York City giving a speech and won't be home until tomorrow morning. We can't wait that long because she'll start to stink, and it would take a whole gang of people to dig a hole for her. And no one wants to do it. So you need to bring the backhoe. I'm sure Professor James will pay for it. I know he would want her to be buried. You're always saying you need jobs for that thing so people will get used to having it around. This job is perfect. But we better get going. This is an emergency! How long will it take you to dig the hole?"

Johnny thought about it. He knew that Charlie was

hardheaded when an idea took hold of him, everyone knew that. But it was the truth that it would be a good way for people to see the backhoe in action. If he did it, he and Charlie would pass the store and people would notice them and want to come and watch old Bat get buried by the wonderful new machine . . .

ACTUALLY, THEY STOPPED at the store for a soda. Charlie was getting anxious but Johnny insisted. It was like advertising. Charlie had taken his shoes off the minute he got into the dump truck, so when he walked into the store, he looked normal except for his color, which was too pale. Johnny started telling folks what was happening. Mr. Dudley poked his head around the corner of the room and listened, glancing back and forth between Charlie and Johnny. He hardly ever left the store/post office, but he always knew what was going on.

It was one-fifteen when they drove up the lane to the Corn House, past the rock where Charlie had seen the dogs kill the doe. It was a tight fit for a dump truck.

Matthew had gotten back with five bags of dairy feed for the milk cow at one o'clock. He drove the pickup down to the little milking barn to unload. As he was finishing, he heard a tractor start up. He thought it must be the echo from Mill Creek Farm, which was owned by rich people from the north and had big tractors. By the time he got back to the gate, he knew it was no echo. When he was halfway down the lane from the big house to the Corn House, he saw the backhoe with Johnny in his aviator glasses taking up the first bucketful of dirt. Off to the right he saw three pickups and a jeep coming up the lane past the rock.

As Matthew got to the foot of the hill, Gretchen called from the house to find out what was going on.

"Nothing wrong, Miz Lewis, we're just burying old Bat. That's all."

Matthew broke into a trot, and at fifty yards he started yelling, something he never did. He seldom used bad language either.

"Charlie Lewis, what in hell are you doing? And where did you get that goddamn backhoe?"

Charlie looked up at Matthew and for a second was scared. But he knew Matthew's broad face in all its looks, and after a glance he knew for sure that it would be all right. Matthew would let it happen. And even though he was almost twelve and had shot up to five foot four over the spring, Charlie took hold of Matthew's sleeve once again. So they watched—there in the unused garden patch with the sun high in the early summer sky and the multiflora rose and honeysuckle coming to bloom and the paradise trees in full leaf overhead.

Johnny dug, and piled the dirt on the side opposite from Bat. The tractor belched away as the throttle governor cut in and out.

By quarter of two, there were twenty people, black and white, standing in the lane watching. No one crossed the old barbed-wire fence into the garden patch for a closer look.

Then Robert Paine and Leonard drove up in Mr. Dudley's pickup. Mr. Dudley might not leave the post office himself, but when Robert came running down across the railroad because he had heard the news, Mr. Dudley told him where Leonard was and to go get him and get up there to see what was happening. Leonard was so excited that he danced across the garden patch as if he were on hot coals. "What's going on, Matthew?" he demanded harshly.

Now people didn't talk to Matthew like that no matter what their color or position. People just didn't yell at Matthew Tanner. But Leonard did then. For him the insanity of the whole affair had boiled down to that one scene. Leonard said that at the time he thought Matthew had gone out of his head.

"Where did that machine come from? That is my dead, one-eyed mule laying there, and I didn't tell nobody they could come in here and bury her with no huge machine and Johnny Griggs running it." He had just as well have spit into the wind, and he knew it the minute he saw Charlie hanging on to Matthew's sleeve.

Robert was grinning. "Matthew," he said, "that white boy done turned your head clean around. Who on God's earth would think of burying some old mule except Charlie Lewis? And you're letting him do it."

The hole was six feet deep and seven feet long and four feet wide. It had taken forty-five minutes to dig.

Johnny glanced over at Charlie as he swung the bucket across the mule's body so that he could push her into the hole. He took off his aviator's glasses.

Charlie nodded.

Bat's body was very close to the edge. Gently the bucket pushed sideways against her. And then she fell in. She hit the bottom with a loud thud. She gave her final whistle as the air was driven from her lungs by the fall. Charlie looked over the edge at her legs sticking up and her head and neck skewed to the side.

Drawn by the crowd, Gretchen had come out from the house in time to see the old mule pushed into the hole. She gasped in horror and started toward Charlie. There was a stillness in the air. Not a sound. Johnny had turned off the tractor. Not a bird. Something in Charlie's look made his mother stop before she got to him. "Charlie, why do you do these things? Why didn't you just let the men take her away and forget her. There was no reason—why, Charlie? . . ." Her voice trailed off.

Charlie's face suddenly went dead white. And then, as if to the whole group—to all of us—he shouted, "Because I loved her!"

A flight of mourning doves came over and landed in the barn lot. And the only sound left in the early summer afternoon was their cooing.

This time in a whisper, he said again: "Because I loved her."

• • •

THE PROFESSOR ARRIVED the next morning on the train from New York City. He was struck nearly speechless when Matthew told the tale.

"Does Johnny Griggs really think that he is going to be paid?" the professor demanded. "And what about Charlie? What is to be done with Charlie, gallivanting off to town and committing me to pay to have a twenty-five-year-old one-eyed mule buried? Really, Matthew, it is too much!" The professor was chuckling in his wheezy way. "And why didn't you stop it? Don't tell me that boy fooled you. You knew all the time what he was doing. It is so unlike you, Matthew . . ."

Then Matthew, in the confidence of their old, old relationship said, "I'm glad he did it. I don't know why, but I'm glad. It was like burying that old mule made the end time of mules. I don't reckon we'll ever see a mule on this farm again. I never did much like mules, but . . ."

CHARLIE GRIEVED AND time went on. A lot of people had seen the backhoe in action, and the professor even paid Johnny the twenty-five dollars. Johnny said that if it hadn't been for Charlie and Bat, heaven knows if he would have ever got that machine off the ground. But off it went. There were houses to build and he began to dig drain fields, too. Farms got cut up. Eventually the company Mr. Lewis worked for moved to town and brought jobs.

There were no more mules at Silver Hill. The following spring Leonard bought a tractor—a Farmall, Model C, used. But it plowed the gardens just fine. Professor James signed the note.

Winter came and it snowed. And as usual, in the evenings, people stood around the potbelly at the store, talking. The tale of the wild dogs was told again. Then silence. Just the sizzling of the fire, and the crack of the expanding cast iron. And then a muffled chuckle as Robert Paine remembered Bat's burial. "It was the craziest thing I ever seen. Even for that Charlie Lewis. And him getting you into it, Matthew. I still can't believe you went along. And the professor, too."

Matthew didn't answer. He stood quietly next to the stove, his face turned away into the shadow. It was as if the events themselves were already beyond comment, as if they had passed into a realm of remembrance where they stood alone, of their own strength. His leather baseball cap was pushed back on his head and his eyes were fixed on something beyond the store.

Robert shook his head, still amazed. His gesture just about covered it. Because not one of us had ever heard of someone loving a mule before.

Foxfire

CHARLIE HAD A WAY of focusing heavily on whatever was his interest of the moment. Anyone could see that. It was as if he had tunnel vision. But it was a mistake to believe that he was blocking out the rest of the world. He could suddenly shift his attention and you'd realize he'd had been absorbing everything around him all the time.

The August he was twelve, he shifted his attention from Matthew and Silver Hill to Luke Henry and his hounds. Charlie had, of course, been along on the hunt for the wild dogs the previous winter, and he had been possum hunting with Luke a few times at night. But he had never shown any special interest in the hounds. He liked dogs—Charlie liked all animals— but that was all.

Luke lived with his wife on seven acres on the back side of Owens Mountain. They lived in a log cabin that his daddy—who had been slave born—had built by hand at the turn of the century. With the exception of a little grove of oaks, the property had originally been covered in mature field pines, which is where the logs for the cabin came from. Tightly chinked, the cabin was almost fifty feet long and divided into three sections. The main one on the end had a massive chimney built with rock hauled up the mountain on sledges pulled by workhorses. That room was the kitchen and living room. The cabin was in a little grove of oaks so there was shade in the summer.

There was a privy close to the porch, with its clay path worn smooth and hard. There were hog pens below the house. If the wind was blowing in your face when you approached the pens, the smell would nearly knock you down. All the small landowners and farmers, black and white, kept hogs. Hogs were the difference between living and what we thought was living well.

Next to the house, just past the privy, there were three pens where Luke kept his hounds. He was the only one in the area who had hounds. They had to be fed, of course, but Luke had inherited them from his daddy along with the place, and he couldn't imagine life without them.

Luke was the section foreman on the C & O Railroad and made more money than any other black man in the community. He was tall and erect and wore khakis summer and winter. In the winter he wore that red-and-black lumber jack coat and hat, and those tall boots with his pants tucked in. When he stood next to the potbelly in the store he was half a head taller than everyone else. Quiet. When he and Matthew Tanner happened to be talking, people stood away so as not to bother them. They were the most important men in the black community. Truth be told, maybe in ours, too. When the deer started to come back after the war, Luke and Matthew were the first two hunters to bring down a buck. No one was surprised at this.

Luke's four sons were gone. Two were in the army, and the other two had jobs in town and lived there. So Luke and his wife, Jessie, who, like many of the black ladies, worked for a white family in the village, were alone at the homeplace. None of the sons showed much interest in Luke's way of life. As quick as they could, they left. It was a loving family, but by this time things had begun to change and the boys wanted no part of the old ways. Using the colored bathrooms at the depot did not suit them. Of course, they soon discovered that they had to use the colored bathrooms in town, but at least there they didn't have to live with the peace that Luke and Jessie had made with Jim Crow.

ONE SATURDAY MORNING in the late August heat, Charlie appeared at Luke's out of the blue, riding his pony. He tied the pony to a locust sapling at the edge of the clearing. Luke and Jessie were sitting on the porch, which was on the side of the log house looking out at the valley. It was lucky that Charlie found them sitting because, by nature, they hardly ever did. Luke said later that in spite of knowing Charlie since he was little, the presence of the fair-skinned, gray-eyed boy with his almost white hair, walking across his own dirt yard shocked him. Most people felt that way about Charlie. He was so pale he looked like he was from somewhere else, maybe somewhere in the Scandinavian countries, the north lands, like Gretchen, his mother.

"Morning, Jessie . . . Luke," he said as he nodded to each in turn. Then there was silence, unusual for Charlie. He looked down at the ground. What was happening was that Charlie had made up his mind that come hell or high water he was going to get near Luke's hounds. He wanted to so badly he was afraid he might say the wrong thing and mess it all up. So for a moment, he was absolutely out of character, speechless.

"Are you going possum hunting tonight, Luke?"

"I reckon so," replied Luke, who saw right away what was going on. "You want to come, Charlie?"

"Yes sir." And then Charlie started off in his regular headlong way of talking. Fast, as if the conversation were an emergency. "Will you turn loose from the summerhouses? Maybe we could jump a fox and not a slow old possum and run him into the swamp below the lake. And then the hounds would run in there all night long and we could sit on the dam and listen.

Maybe Matthew would come. And my daddy, too. He is home this weekend."

"Sure, Charlie." Luke was smiling all over his narrow face. "We'll turn loose from the summerhouses, but I don't want the hounds running no fox if I can help it. It's too hard getting them off. And I don't want to stay up all night long when I got to get ready for church in the morning, and worrying about them all during the sermon—though"—here he paused and glanced slyly at Jessie—"sometimes it's more interesting to listen to the hounds . . ."

"Now Luke, don't you talk that way in front of Charlie. He'll get us wrong about church." But she was smiling, too. And they both kept rocking easily in the split cane chairs, in the August heat.

That evening, Luke brought the hounds in their crates in his old pickup to the foot of the lane to the burnt-out summerhouses. Immediately it became clear that Charlie had found his new thing. Even before they turned loose, he started out talking almost nonstop. Question upon question, until Luke got disgusted at not being able to listen for the hounds. He said to Matthew, "Can't you keep that boy quiet?"

"It's pretty hard, Luke, once he gets going."

Finally his daddy spoke to him. "Now Charlie, you be quiet and listen or we are going home. Keep your questions for Luke till you see him during the day. We're out here to listen to the hounds, not you!"

So Charlie shut up and the hounds ran, above the lake in the oaks, their voices echoing through the woods with the long trailing note of treeing night hounds. There were eight of them. Five dogs and three bitches, all black and tans, with ears long enough to stretch beyond their noses if you pulled them forward and dark eyes that looked like they had seen everything in the world at least three times over. And considering the bags underneath their eyes, you would wonder if they had ever closed them—ever slept. Solemn-looking. Gentle. Sometimes a little shy.

When they came over a ridge running toward you, throwing their tongues all together, your breath got short and the hair on the back of your neck rose up and you knew you were listening to something awful old. And it didn't matter where you came from or what color you were.

They quickly treed a possum. Matthew and Luke knew they had treed when the note of their voices changed—it became quick and staccato, more like barking than the long, baying note they used when they were running the track. Charlie and the men ran through the thick woods and got to the tree short of breath. Matthew searched for the possum with a big flashlight, and finally they saw him. A big one— a boar, his eyes reflecting red in the light, looking down on them. Luke moved around the tree trying to get a clear shot with the old Winchester .22 pump. But the possum kept moving around also. Finally he stopped.

"You want to take a shot at him, Mr. Lewis?" Luke asked. "I reckon he'll be a long sight easier to hit than that bat I heard about you killed in church with the short-short."

Charlie's father might have been an outlander from Pennsylvania, but as you know, he was a sure shot with a .22. He had killed the bat in church because the thing kept flying around at evening prayer and scaring the ladies.

"Sure, I'll give it a try, Luke," Charlie's daddy said. He was in his early thirties then, skinny, and as dark as Charlie was fair. But they both had the hawk nose that was said to have descended to them from far-off male ancestors. Charles's job often kept him away during the week on business, and he didn't share Charlie's passion for everything to do with the countryside. He was, however, an understanding presence backing up Charlie's life. It was a good time for them.

Charles took off his glasses and hitched himself around as was his habit. Eased out his breath. The hounds sat looking up. Their ancient eyes having seen it all centuries before, they were still mildly interested —even though they ran for the running, not the killing. Then the crack of the long rifle hollow point. Matthew held steady with the light. The possum jerked, but did not fall.

"Let me go up and get him!" Charlie gasped out the instant the possum jerked. "Let me go, Luke!"

Luke glanced at Charles, who smiled and nodded. And Charlie was off up the tree. Climbing through the limbs of the white pine as fast as he could.

"Now you watch him, Charlie," called Matthew.

"You don't have no idea is he dead or not. If he grabs you with those fox jaws, he could halfway bite your thumb off."

Charlie climbed, a pale presence in the shadowy branches of the pine. As he climbed, the three men below glanced at each other, bemused by the boy. Matthew smiled and shook his head a little.

"I'm up here!" hollered Charlie.

"We see! We see!" said his father.

"Shake him out, Charlie!" yelled Luke. "Shake the branch. Is he dead?"

"He's dead. He ain't moving."

"Not ain't, isn't," said his father automatically as he returned the rifle to Luke.

"Okay, isn't," replied Charlie.

The possum fell then, crashing through the branches and hitting the ground with a thud. The hounds focused on him, just to be positive he was dead, which he wasn't. When the possum moved, Luke brought up the rifle in a smooth motion and fired. The head jerked, and that was all.

Just as Charlie reached the ground, a sudden closed look came on his face. He jumped to Matthew's side.

"Why did we have to shoot him?"

"So Luke and Jessie can have roast possum, Charlie. Pork's about gone and it's still a long time to hog killing," said Matthew. "Anyway, that's the way we do it. We all like to hear the hounds run. The hounds like it. We like it. And Luke and Jessie get dinner."

The look passed from Charlie's face as quickly as it had come.

"I know," he said.

THE NEXT DAY, as soon as Sunday dinner was over, Charlie asked if he could ride over to Owens Mountain to see Luke. Gretchen wasn't sure.

"What if the Henrys haven't finished their dinner, Charlie?"

"They'll be finished by the time I get there. It takes forty-five minutes on the pony, Gretchen," said Charlie.

Charlie, like everyone else in the community, called her Gretchen. She was the pale, fair, grown-up female version of Charlie. She had never lived in the country before, and so she was often frightened for him. But she trusted Matthew. And even though his daddy was gone during the week, she was sure that in spite of his various adventures, Charlie would probably survive to adulthood as long as Matthew and, to a lesser extent, Professor James, were watching over the situation.

"All right then. Go on. But mind your manners and be back before dark."

The rector of the church was at the Lewises' for Sunday lunch. He knew Charlie, too. "What's he doing? Getting ready to go wild over Luke's possum hounds?" he asked.

"I guess so," replied Charlie's father. "He seems to go from one thing to the other. And those hounds seem to be the next thing. Considering some of his other 'things,' this one seems pretty safe. Although you can't tell." He smiled.

Just as Charlie knew they'd be, Luke and Jessie were on the porch in their rockers. Luke had changed into his khaki work clothes, but Jessie was still dressed for church fanning herself with a split-cane fan. The kind found in all the churches, black and white.

"Jessie . . . Luke, good afternoon." Charlie made his manners.

The boy and the man stepped over to the hound pens. Jessie, whose granddaddy was said to have been an Indian and whose cheekbones, as a result, looked as if they had been chiseled from solid rock, looked on from the porch, fanning and thinking, *When it comes to dogs and hunting, men ain't got good sense. At least my man don't. He'd rather spend the whole night hunting for one possum, which ain't that good to eat nohow, spend all night long just to hear the dogs run—and then traipsing up and down the country looking for lost ones . . . And look at that Charlie Lewis. He'll catch it sure enough. And next thing you know he'll . . .* Suddenly, she said aloud, "Charlie Lewis, where is your hat? You'll take a heat stroke sure enough out there with no hat on, and you fair as you is . . ." She tramped into the house and emerged with a battered old felt hat with a band of ribbon and a little quail feather in the band and said, "Now Charlie, you put this hat on, and I hope you turn out to have more sense than the man it belongs to." Smiling.

And Luke smiled back. "Old lady, what you talking about sense. You know I got more sense than mighty near anyone you ever knowed. This boy wants to learn. So I'll teach him."

Into the sultry afternoon the man talked and the boy listened, his eyes moving from hound to man and back as he took in the lore of the black and tans: their names and their sires' and dams' names, and the great hunts—Luke sometimes called them races—they'd been on. Like the time the hounds—there were ten that night—jumped a fox over next to Quail Hill. The men didn't mean to run a fox because there was no telling how the hunt would end up. Sometimes a fox would carry them all the way to Greenwood—or the other way, to the town. Once the hounds got running, they usually couldn't be stopped, what with them going kind of crazy and the men, too, for that matter, it was so exciting. On that night, him and William Critzer and Sammy Jones were at the foot of the mountain, downwind, as the fox come over, heading straight at them. And old Belle . . .

And here the narrative came to a pause. "That's her granddaughter there—that gyp with the split ear—do you see, Charlie? Do you see her?

"Yes sir, I see her—right there. What's her name?"

"Why, Sarah, Charlie. Name Sarah. Ain't she lovely? Small—but look at her beautiful feet. And legs. And her so smooth and silkylike. She ain't but a second-year bitch, but, oh Lord, she done got good already.

She can strike a cold track while the rest just standing around. And go on with it, too. Ain't no dwelling with her. No sir . . . Call her, Charlie. She'll come to you. She's gentle as can be."

Jessie saw it happen from the porch. Saw the boy look at the little black and tan bitch, and call her name and her come to him, saw him look at her eyes and then, as she came to him, draw back slightly as if startled, as if he were connecting to a creature completely new to him. She saw him reach out to touch her, with his palm down. And saw her lower her head a little. And then she heard Luke's voice—"No, Charlie, not like that. Put your palm up. Let her smell of your palm. If you go at her the other way, she'll think you threatening her. See how gentle she is?" Jessie watched Charlie put his hand under her jaw and still looking at her, sit on a stump, and Sarah lay her head on his leg.

The scene froze. Jessie gently rocking, was wrapped, a little sadly, in all the accumulated scenes of men and hounds, over all the years. Luke was lost in the tale itself, not even speaking it now. The skinny white boy sat on the stump, the head of the beautiful little black-and-tan bitch in his lap, taking up the story as if to give color to his pale skin.

"But then what happened, Luke?"

"Why, Charlie, they come off the mountain just flying. Covered that half mile in nothing flat. And us standing there holding our breath—standing in the little clearing next to the branch." Luke was talking

faster in the urgency of the tale. "And there he was—
a big red, but real dark, almost black, and strong looking, with no white hairs on his tail. I recollect him
still. What he looked like . . . He saw us and slammed
on the brakes. He just stopped and sat down, his
tongue hanging out. He looked back over his shoulder
at where he come from. Then gone and them ten
hounds come into the clearing running wide open.
Not one of 'em looked up, throwing their tongues like
great God Almighty, and straight on after that fox,
down the branch and skirting the lake and into the
swamp. Then I knowed we was for it."

"Why, Luke? What's wrong with the swamp?"

"Hush, Charlie! I'm telling you! Well, anyway,
William—even back then William wasn't getting
around too good, he was so fat—William said, 'Luke,
I reckon we'd better get the trucks. Cause the way I
am, I won't be able to get to the lake by daybreak,
walking.' So William and Sammy jump into William's
truck, and followed me down to the village and then
back through Silver Hill, and down to the lake.

"And not a sound. Not one peep out of a hound
and us standing on the dam looking out at the swamp
in the moonlight, and lightning bugs shining and
every tree frog in creation yelling at once. But not a
sound from a hound.

"And Sammy Jones—him and his brother run their
daddy's dairy over to the reservoir—You know them,
don't you, Charlie?"

"Yes sir, I know them."

"Well, anyway, Sammy says, 'Luke, The way them dogs'—Sammy always used to call 'em 'dogs'—'was pouring it to him coming off the mountain at Quail Hill, I bet they run that fox right through the whole swamp, out the other side past Mill Creek Farm, maybe clean to Locust Hill.' You see, Charlie, Sammy was always one of them fellers what expected the worst on a hunt. Either we'd loose the hounds clear across the Ragged Mountains, or they'd get hit on Route 280—always something. Sammy was like William—too fat. But Sammy had a great ear for a race: when they were in hearing, Sammy could tell you just who was doing what in the hunt. Even when the hounds weren't his. Yes, Sammy has about the best ear of any white man I ever knowed.

"Well, just as we figured Sammy was right and we were heading for the trucks, here they come back again. On the far side of the swamp. And you didn't need to be no expert to hear old Belle's high chop carrying that hunt. She was throwing everything she had to that fox's trail, and the rest coming along right behind her.

"It sure was grand to hear. We figured the fox would settle down and stay in the swamp and go round and round—what with the hounds having to wallow along in the mud and water—with the fox just jumping from hummock to hummock. So we sat down on the dam to listen, and William pulled out a pint of store-bought white man's whiskey and everybody took a pull. Not that I got anything against store-bought whiskey, but the Smith boys up the hollow—"

Jessie had been listening with half an ear, and jumped in. "Luke, don't you be talking to that boy about no whiskey, store-bought or otherwise. You hear?"

Before Luke could reply, Charlie asked, "Where did the swamp come from, Luke? Matthew said something about another lake, but . . ."

"That's what it started out. Way back. Old man Brighten built the first lake, the one still there. Right where the rock ledge would be a spillway. It worked fine. So he thought he'd build him another one, below the first one. But that dam was long and there weren't no rock spillway. So come the hurricane in '26, and water poured over the rock spillway into the second lake and water ran over top that dirt dam and the whole thing washed away. Washed down to two foot high. And the trees and grass just growed right up in there, till it was a swamp. Sometimes in drought it about dries up—just the creek in the middle keeps running, and everthing else dries up. The old cow path is still beside the creek, what was always there, even when the rest is swamp. So you can get through straight along the creek. Actually, you can look along it the whole way from the upper end. Ain't you ever been in there, Charlie?"—But he only stopped long enough to draw breath and went on—"And that was the only time I ever seen foxfire. Right along that path."

And then Charlie said, "But what happened next on the hunt? What did the fox do, Luke? Did you see him again?" Charlie knew what foxfire was. But he didn't know how the hunt would end.

"Well, they crossed the Mill Creek road coming right at us, coming up the path next to the creek. And then we seen it. A glowing trail—patches of it—like drawing a line on a paper, only this line glowing like fire, coming right at us. And straight up the dam it come. And there was the fox again. Leaving a trail of light with his feet where he'd stepped into the foxfire mushrooms and carried the pieces along with him. But no stopping this time. No sir! Rolling on up the hill on the other side of the dam, straight back to Quail Hill. Leaving the foxfire trail behind. And then here come the ten hounds up the cow path and all of a sudden the whole path lit up again with foxfire where the hounds run into what the fox left behind.

"And us speechless! Never in my life did I see William Critzer without something to say—"

Here Jessie jumped in again. "Or you either, old man. And I still ain't heard you without something to say about a hunt." As she rocked, smiling, on the porch. But not even Jessie could stop Luke now.

"So we set on the dam and took another pull as the foxfire give out, and the hounds run on behind that fox. Back to Quail Hill like we thought, and then turned to come back again. And William said we'd sure as hell better stop them hounds if they come back through, cause he didn't want to see that glowing trail down through the swamp again."

"Was William scared, Luke? Did the foxfire scare him? Did it scare you?"

"No, I reckon not. Weren't none of us scared, really. We'd all heard of it. But it seemed like such a old-timey thing. Something long out of memory. Something the old people saw. Not us. But we did see it, for a fact . . . for a fact." And here he paused. Stopped. His eyes got distance in them. And Charlie's, too, as if he somehow was remembering the story, as if he had been there that night and seen the foxfire, or dreamed it.

A crow called in the dreamy heat. Sarah raised her head from Charlie's knee and yawned. The spell was broken.

"Well, that fox run right on to Quail Hill, doubled, and come straight back on his first track. Laying one trail on top of the other. But the hounds knowed they wont backtracking. So they rolled right on towards us. And then come the fox, again. But we didn't say nothing. Once he passed, all of us got out the couplings and stood across the fox's track, spread out and ready. So when Belle come out of the woods, I grabbed her and hooked on the coupling and then little Star and hooked her on the other end. Hook two hounds together like that and they're easier to handle. William and Sammy got two apiece, so we had the lead hounds. The four puppies stopped to be friendly. They weren't a hundred percent sure what was going on, anyway. So we caught 'em all. And glad we had. Cause that was enough for one night. We stood still for a minute. The hounds panting, and us, too, for that matter. Clouds come up. Fixing to rain. Time to go."

"But Luke, did the fox leave the foxfire trail that time through the swamp?"

"I don't know. Didn't none of us look over his shoulder."

"But why not, Luke? Didn't you want to know?"

"I reckon we was too busy getting ready to catch the hounds . . . We just didn't look . . . that's all . . ." Luke's words trailed off.

Suddenly, in the tension of the moment, Charlie burst out in his high, urgent voice, "But I want to know, Luke. I want to. I want to see the foxfire trail when the fox comes through and hear Sarah's high voice carrying the hunt, and when they come back the second time, I'll watch to see if the trail glows again, and I'll let the hounds run on all night long, and I'll go into the swamp, too . . . to see what happens. I'm going to do that, Luke. I know I will, won't I?"

Jessie abruptly stopped fanning, and Luke's eyes settled sharp on Charlie. Sarah, feeling the mood, looked up at the boy's pale face, with Luke's old felt hat shading his forehead. And then Jessie, her chiseled face taut, not smiling and the fan not moving, said, "Is that why you telling this boy this story, old man? So he can set on some dam all night long, listening and watching for something that ain't going to happen, thinking them hound voices got something to say that he got to hear? Is that it?"

A shadow passed across Luke's face. And then was gone. "I reckon so, Jessie," he said, smiling again. "I reckon so."

Gray Vixen

THE HUNTING WAS GOOD that winter. Charlie, who would be thirteen the following summer, went on Saturday nights. He and the hound, Sarah, grew close. He would let the tailgate down on the truck and put his hand through the wire mesh in the hound-box doors, and she would lick his fingers and wiggle while he smiled and called her name.

Several times they chased a coon. It had been roughly a decade since the coons had suddenly disappeared. It was in the fall of the first year of the war. Not one had been seen since. Until now. After the first one, when the hounds treed, the men shone the flashlights into the tree to be completely sure what was up there. On the occasions when a coon's wide-set eyes and masked face looked down on them, the

men cheered. And the coon was let alone to run another day, and breed at the season's end.

One night Luke Henry told Charlie in his matter-
of-fact voice what had happened those ten years ago
when the coons disappeared. "We killed 'em all off. It
was greed. Just too much running."

Here he paused, looking backward. Then went on
quietly, "They sure do run good. Give the hounds fits.
And taste good, too. They got faces. Not like a possum.
A possum looks like a witch. The coon is your friend."

After that, each night had a special sense of antic-
ipation. Would this be the one when again they would
meet the face of their friend, the coon? By chance,
each time they did, Charlie was there and wanting to
climb the tree to get a closer look at the coon's quizzical face. But Luke told Charlie just what a mature
boar coon could do to *his* face with the long claws in
the shape of hands. They had begun to see prints of
those hands again last summer along certain creek
banks where the crawfish hunting was good.

Only once during the whole winter had they run a
fox. She was a gray vixen who came off Quail Hill one
night and ran into the swamp below the lake. But not
before they had seen her in the light of their big flashlights. She was heavy with young, and her body was
the gray-speckled color of guinea hens with red guard
hairs stretching from her long nose to her hips. She
was a contrast in color. She was much larger than the
red foxes Charlie had seen—and very beautiful. She
simply disappeared.

"She got a den in there somewhere," Luke said. "Likely in a hollow tree. Most times when a gray goes in, the hounds won't say nothing when they tree in the ground. They just don't like running a gray for some reason. She'll have her young in there. Probably never see her again. Grays are funny. They don't want to run. They stay out of the way. Some people say they's a cat cause they climb trees sometimes. But they ain't. Got feet just like a red . . ."

Charlie wanted to pursue the subject. He wanted to pursue every subject. But Luke didn't have anything more to say about gray foxes. We called them red-sided grays. They were a mystery.

By the end of the season, when the hunting stopped to let the creatures produce their young, Charlie, after a fall and winter of endless questions and yearnings and outbreaks of enthusiasm, had got it. In spite of the talk—and without thought—he had begun to understand the need to be with hounds.

If an outsider had asked why he liked it, Charlie would have given the standard hunter's response to the question. It would have been staged in imitation of Luke. Charlie would turn his head aside, look at the ground, and say, in a deferential voice, with just the right inflection, "Oh, I just like to hear the dogs run."

Then he would glance up to see the approval on Luke's face at the handling of the secret—and the confusion or downright derision on the face of the questioner. It never seemed to go any further. The "why" was never asked.

Actually, for most of us, Charlie's explanation was almost the answer, leave out the mystery. Nobody would starve without possums to eat, and it cost money to feed hounds, not to mention the aggravation to wives and mothers. But everyone agreed it was grand to hear the hounds' voices on a cloudy winter night. Very few people had hounds anymore. Luke was the only one in the area, leaving out the hunt club, which kept a big pack of hounds for the people to follow on horseback during the day.

And so the season ended. Summer came and Luke, to the total disgust of Jessie, bought three Plott hounds.

"What in heaven's name"—Jessie thought a lot about heaven when it came to hounds—"do you need with three more dogs in that pen, Luke?" she demanded.

"You know I need three fast dogs to chase the coons now they coming back," he replied, looking suitably guilty. "Plenty of scraps from the school to feed three more hounds. Maybe a bear will come down out of the mountain. You know Plotts will tree anything. I got to be ready . . ." The conversation went around in a circle, utterly predictable, as was the outcome.

So the new hounds arrived. Big brindle-colored dogs with ears Charlie thought too short, and hard expressions on their faces, unlike Sarah who was soft and loving. The first Saturday night they dug out of the pen and proceeded to go on a rampage through the whole countryside, running a fox clear from Owens Mountain to the edge of town and back. Half the village heard at least some part of it. Luke came for Charlie first thing and Gretchen let him go. She knew Luke was in a fever to get back in touch with the hounds.

"When I left 'em, they was on the other side of Owens Mountain," he said, letting the old truck careen around the country roads. Just as they turned onto Owens Road, Luke slammed on the brakes and leaned out of the window. "Listen, Charlie, they's heading for Silver Hill. That fox is aimed for town. Been years since a fox run all the way to town." So they rushed to Mill Creek Farm to intercept them. Sure enough, here came the hounds. Headed straight for the little mountain at the edge of the town. And so it went, crossing after crossing. Twice they arrived soon enough to see the fox coming through. Luke drove his old truck like a maniac.

Charlie was beside himself with joy. "How do you always know where the fox will run, Luke? How do you know?" His exuberant questions came insistent and unrelenting.

Luke started to sum up his answers at one point, saying, "My daddy told me about one time . . ." But the story was too long to tell in the middle of this hunt, so he dropped it. For once Charlie was too engrossed in the present to pursue the past, so he let it go, too.

It went on most of the night—the two loops

around Owens Mountain, then six miles to town, six miles back, and two more loops around the mountain before the fox had had enough and gone to ground.

The next evening there was a rehash of the hunt at the store. Luke's brother, Fred, allowed as how he never heard such awful hound voices in his life. "They sound like feists to me, Luke. Yip-yippin' along. But Lord, they are fast. I never heard hounds run through country like that. It's a wonder they didn't catch that fox. Would have, too, if it hadn't of been that old dog fox from the other side of Owens Mountain—but they sure don't sing! No sir, they don't sing."

Luke worked on the pen. He put cinder blocks all along the base of the wire to keep the hounds from digging out. They tried, but couldn't. It looked like the answer. Finally he put them in with the other grown hounds. Summer went on, and then August, and time to start thinking about hunting when the weather broke.

On a particularly sultry afternoon—sultry in a way only central Virginia on an August afternoon can be—Matthew Tanner and Charlie were working on the old pasture fence halfway up the lane to the burnt-out summerhouses. Charlie, who had just turned thirteen, spent all the time he could with Matthew, who knew the things about the country and farms that Charlie almost desperately needed to know.

The fence was pitiful. It seemed to be held up by honeysuckle and multiflora rose vines. The cows worked every inch of it looking for a weak place where the wire had come loose from the locust posts. When a cow found one, she marched right through. And then here came the rest, like buzzards congregating at a dead animal. Out and gone. Then Matthew would have to find Ellis Breeden, who rented the pasture, to come and get the cows back in before they ruined the gardens. And then he'd have to patch the fence.

"Why doesn't Professor James build a new one, Matthew?" Charlie asked. "Doesn't he have enough money?"

"Oh, he got plenty of money. It ain't that. It's just that"—and here there was a pause—"well, you know him and Miz James don't have no children. And when they die, the farm goes to the university." Here Matthew picked up speed as if to get it over with. "And the university ain't going to farm seven hundred acres. Which means the place will get cut up . . . So it don't make no sense to build new fences if it ain't going to be a farm." Matthew was almost out of breath from the unaccustomed onslaught of words. He looked sidewise at the white-haired boy next to him, almost in guilt, as Charlie, of course, asked, "Why?"

Sarah's high voice saved Matthew from the answer—hers and those of the other twelve hounds who were with her, running wide open in the August oppression. The sound was coming from behind the summerhouses, from Joe Stephens's farm and, from there, Owens Mountain.

"Lord, they done escaped again!" Matthew caught his breath. "But I don't hear the Plotts. Do you, Charlie?"

Charlie by this time was beside himself at the day-light sound of the hounds' voices, and at Sarah carry-ing the hunt in the heat, though the other deeper voices were right with her. They headed for the lake.

"No Plotts in there," yelled Charlie with his usual confidence. "I know all those voices." It was true. He did know all those voices.

Matthew and Charlie raced to the other side of the road and clambered over the risky fence in time to see the pack burst into view from the mature oak forest at the top of the hill. Running as if it were a cold winter night when your breath makes steam in front of you, not cotton in the lungs. They both looked down the long meadow toward the lake, searching for the quarry —from the pace, necessarily a fox. Nothing else ex-cept a deer could run in front of those hounds like that without being caught in the first field. They would have seen the deer. But where was the fox?

"Do you see him, Matthew? I don't see nothing," asked Charlie, lapsing into the speech of his compan-ions, which Gretchen disapproved of and would not countenance in the house. This was of little matter to Charlie, who quickly developed two different languages —one for home and the other for the rest of the time, even though Matthew tried to back up Gretchen.

"Don't talk like that, Charlie. I don't see nothing ei-ther. Must be in this heat the fox got a good lead on the hounds. Maybe scent ain't holding." He studied the woods edge next to the lake, expecting to see the pale flame of a red fox melt into the swamp.

But there was nothing. The hounds came across the field still running hard in spite of the heat and disappeared along with their voices into the swamp. Then silence. Just nothing!

"Where—," began Charlie.

"Hush a minute, Charlie. Hush! There be a loss. We'll hear 'em again in a second."

But they didn't. Not for five minutes on Matthew's Little Ben pocket watch. And suddenly there was an urgency to know, a suspense like the thickening of the air before an August storm. Matthew felt it, and Charlie was in a knot. The tree line into the swamp was suddenly a barrier before another world. A world that had swallowed up Sarah whole, not to mention the other hounds.

"We got to find Luke. Come on, Charlie! I think he's down to Stevens Crossing lining track. Ought to be just about finished by now. Come on!"

"No! Let me stay and look. You go. I'll walk down the cow path in the swamp. Maybe something awful has happened. And Sarah . . . !" And Charlie started down the hill at a run, jumping clumps of broom sage, his arms flung out, already hollering for her, "Sarah! Sarah!"

Matthew turned toward the truck. The boy would be all right. There were no bears in that swamp. And you couldn't see foxfire at three in the afternoon in August. So he went on off in search of Luke.

• • •

LUKE KNEW RIGHT OFF what had happened. There was a little pond in the swamp. And when the hounds crossed it, almost swimming, they sometimes shut up, even if they could still scent the fox on the water's surface. Then at the road, where they would be at a loss for sure, their momentum would carry them forward, across, and into the little dip in the pasture just beyond the Mill Creek fence. So by the time they struck it off again and started throwing their tongues in the August heat, Matthew and Charlie had missed them.

Luke was immediately hot to go to the back of Mill Creek and catch the hounds as they returned from Locust Hill Farm, assuming they could keep the track going in this heat and the fox ran the right way. And he needed Matthew to help him because there were so many hounds.

"But Charlie . . ."

"Charlie goin' to be fine, Matthew. He'll just plow around in the swamp. No harm."

"A cottonmouth—," began Matthew.

"You know there ain't been a cottonmouth seen around here in years, Matthew."

So off they went to Mill Creek. And sure enough, next to the huge manure pile at the back of the farm, they paused, and here came the hounds, running hard, but their voices sounding muffled in the thick, hot air. The fox emerged from the woods with his tongue hanging out and ran right over the top of the steaming, rich-smelling mountain of horse manure.

"Now we'll get 'em. Watch what happens when they try to track across that 'mountain,' Matthew. That fox fooled 'em this time! They won't be able to smell a lick on the manure pile. And by the time they cast around it, we'll have 'em. That was a young fox. He's had enough. He goin' home to the den he was born in cause he still don't know the country."

It was Luke's nature to explain every hunt in detail even if the listener knew perfectly well what was going on, which of course Matthew did. Sometimes the explanations were an aggravation, but often there was some new bit of news to be gotten from the tenth rendition of a repeat occurrence at some stage of a hunt. The stories were difficult. It was hard to think that any one person could explain the whole thing—like scent and all the habits of dogs, let alone foxes. And because Luke was sure everyone wanted to know all there was to know about everything connected with hunting, at times he did tend to go on too long.

The hounds came out of the woods exactly on the fox's track, but when they hit the edge of the manure pile, they stopped short, as if they had run into a solid wall and not the edge of a manure pile. So when Luke called, they all raised their heads and started to wiggle and smile, as if saying how strange it was to see the men there—but nice, too—and what's next?

"Grab 'em, Matthew. String this bale string through the collars. We'll just have to tie 'em in the truck since we ain't got the hound boxes."

Sarah was next to Matthew, panting so hard her

whole body shook. It looked like her tongue would drop out of her head. Suddenly she went rigid all over and fell to the ground, and her eyes rolled back in her head. She was breathing with her mouth shut. Luke was busy tying the other hounds in the truck.

"Luke!" Matthew yelled. It was completely unlike him. Matthew Tanner just didn't yell. At least not often. And when it happened, it almost always had to do with Charlie.

Luke jumped down from the truck and sat on a log next to the truck with the beautiful little bitch in his lap, talking to her, telling her that it would be all right, that she was just having a running fit, that in the heat it happened sometimes with young hounds. He told her he would give her some worm medicine because some said it was worms what caused it. She would be all right in just a minute he said, in a tone of voice loaded with concern, even though he had seen it many times. They almost always came back— almost always.

"Oh my Lord. What would Charlie say?" Matthew said, thinking out loud.

But before he could pursue this totally unacceptable notion, she started to come back, and five minutes later she was okay. Panting again like a normal, overheated dog.

Matthew had to drive so Luke could stay in the back of the truck and be sure none of the hounds could jump out and strangle himself on the bale string.

They parked the truck under the huge old beech tree next to the dam so the hounds would be cool. We called it the loving tree because generations of young people had carved their initials in its soft skin. After a drink in the pond, the hounds didn't fuss against the ties because they were exhausted and happy to be in the shade.

But where was Charlie? They had half expected to see him walking up the lane to the big house when they drove in. It was five o'clock. Gretchen would begin to wonder, although in the summer when Charlie was with Matthew, she never worried much.

Matthew hollered a few times. They started across the north edge of the swamp, through the deep, open woods that separated the home pasture of Silver Hill from the swamp. Almost at the gravel road, they stopped and Matthew yelled again. This time Charlie's raspy voice came back. "Here I am! Here I am!" he called over and over, not scared, but flat, like he was telling the air where he was.

The edge of the swamp was like the edge of a pond with almost no water in it. But it was deep in mud and swamp plants and dead oaks that could not grow in such a place. When Charlie emerged, the men almost burst out laughing. He had no shoes—as was his summer policy. A raggedy Sunday shirt that Gretchen had cut the sleeves off, and blue jeans, with one knee out, were covered in muddy swamp water. His blond hair was a beacon, because he refused to wear a hat.

"Did you find the hounds?"—this in his most urgent voice. "Did you find them?" Smiling just a little. Three times before Luke could get a word in edgewise.

"Sure we found 'em," replied Luke. "What you think, Charlie? You know I know hounds and how the land lays? Sure we found 'em."

There was a pause in the summer air.

"What did you find, Charlie?" Matthew asked.

Suddenly the smile dropped from Charlie's face. And the men stopped, too, because with Charlie you never knew.

"Tell it, Charlie," demanded Matthew, almost harshly. "What happened in there?

Charlie glanced from one to the other. And then in his softest voice, he said, "I found her! . . . In the middle. On a little island—"

"Who, Charlie? Not Sarah. She was with us. Start from the beginning. What happened?"

"I ran down the path through the middle of the swamp, hollering for Sarah, because I thought she would come if she could hear me. Halfway through, I thought I heard something struggle in the swamp. Off to the left. So I went in. But I couldn't find anything. So I kept going. It's deep in there, Matthew. Sometimes I almost had to swim. I wondered about snakes. But I didn't see any. So I kept going. Then there was a little island in front of me. About two feet higher than the swamp. With a big oak in the middle of it and a huge old, dead locust lying on the ground. I came up from the water about level with the land.

"And she was there. Lying on her side, head up, looking at me. Her ears were up and she was panting in the heat. I could see her nipples and the fine hair all around them wet where the babies had been suckling. I saw the eyes of three cubs looking out at me from the hollow locust tree.

"She scared me a little. But her eyes were just like you told me, Luke. They had straight up-and-down slits—like a cat's. Not like Sarah's. I never . . ."

Later, at the store, after many tellings, the tale took on the quality of a painting—The gray vixen mother lying on her side with her young peering out from the hollow locust log, the blond-headed boy rising from the swamp like a character from a story, staring at each other. It was an unlikely scene made more so by the fact that no one had ever heard of a fox having a litter so late that the young would still be suckling in August. It must have been her second litter of the season, because back in January, when they had first seen her, she was heavy, too. But no one questioned the story. Charlie was serious about the truth in stories. He had seen his nursing vixen deep in that August swamp. No one doubted that.

"What did you do then, Charlie?" demanded Luke.

"Well, we looked at each other for a long time. Then I put out my hand. I had the palm up, like you taught me, Luke, so she wouldn't be scared. And then . . ."—looking for words—"and then . . . she . . ."

"What, Charlie? What did she do? Tell it!"

"She put her ears down, flat alongside her head.

Like when a puppy begs. And lowered her head like Sarah did that first day. She looked straight up at me, and for a second . . ."—still searching—"she was soft . . . we were friends.

"But then she reared up on her front legs and pulled her head back and looked at me the way the tan bitch did that day she killed the doe. I couldn't put my hand out any further . . ."

Charlie's gray eyes were wide. "That's what happened. She pulled her head back . . . That's all . . . It was time to go." The three of them stood still then, in the August heat with the mourning doves' incessant cooing.

Until Luke burst out, "Where the hell do you reckon the Plotts got to? They're the ones must of dug out. Do you reckon they went off toward Whitehall on a deer? Come on here! We got to get these hounds home and go after them Plotts."

He was already heading for the truck.

Bobwhite

THE PROBLEM BEGAN WITH SARAH. The black-and-tan bitch would wiggle all over and lick his hand when he came to the hound pen or approached the hound boxes and called her name. In the open she would actually come to him when he called. Even Luke had to head the other hounds off before he could catch most of them. When the hounds were loose, they wanted to hunt, not stand around with humans, but almost from the beginning Sarah would come when Charlie called. The men actually referred to her sometimes as "Charlie's bitch," but she wasn't. After each hunt she loaded up in the hound boxes with the rest of the pack and went home to Owens Mountain, to the pens next to Luke's log cabin.

Charlie mentioned this to Matthew only once. His

answer was short. "She belongs in the pen with the hounds, Charlie. If you had her home and loose, she'd hunt twenty-three hours a day, only stop to eat a little. In a month she'd be skin and bones and ruined." Charlie knew what Matthew said was true. He never brought it up again. But he had that look in his eye that he had when an idea got hold of him. This conversation took place during the fall after Charlie had seen the gray vixen in the swamp.

Casting around for alternatives, Charlie began to look at Uncle Dan, the old English pointer, with different eyes. After all, in his own peculiar way the old pointer also had the gift of scent.

No one knew where Uncle Dan came from originally, but he came to the Lewises from out of their garbage barrel. The handling of garbage was primitive in those days. Most people had a fifty-five-gallon drum with holes in the bottom and sides punched with a cold chisel for ventilation. This barrel was usually kept somewhere out behind the house. The garbage was burned in the barrel. Actually, little else but the paper really burned, so every once in a while the barrel had to be loaded on a pickup and taken to the edge of the mountain behind Quail Hill and dumped right over. Eventually, as the population increased, this solution became a problem. But like a lot of things, we didn't really know any better, so that is what happened. The Lewises kept their barrel in the old cattle chute halfway to the barn. It was convenient and you couldn't see it from the house.

One Sunday morning that fall, Charlie's father took the trash out to the loading chute to burn it. To his surprise the barrel was on its side and protruding from it was the hind end of a dog. Mr. Lewis let out a yell at the mess, and the dog backed out of the barrel. At this point Charlie, who had heard the yell and was coming to find out what was going on, rounded the corner of the loading chute just as the dog turned to look at them with apprehension, aware that they would be furious. One look at the dog told you that hunger's pull had overridden fear, and he was in that barrel for better or worse.

This was no mutt. He was white—or had been—with liver spots and the square, domed head of the English pointer. It was also clear that this dog had been through hell and high water. The last six inches of his tail, which had no hair on it, gave him a certain possumlike aspect. His feet were splayed out with age and wear and tear, and his ears, while not exactly shredded, were certainly not intact. His hipbones stuck up in the air. We never did find out his story.

Charlie crouched to the ground, put out his hand, and made a crooning noise in his throat. The dog looked at Charlie and through some deep understanding of human nature realized that his ship had come in—that his nights in the cold and days of too little food were over. He had found Charlie.

His name was Uncle Dan. Charlie's father named him right then but could not for the life of him figure out why. He just said the dog looked like an Uncle

Dan and that was that. So by the time the old dog got to the house that Sunday morning, he already had a name and Charlie had that look on his face. Gretchen tried to put her foot down. She was not going to let that awful dirty creature in her house. But she was too late. The men in her life had become silent conspirators. She did require, however, that the dog have a bath. This event took place in the old-fashioned bathtub in the Corn House's one bathroom. Uncle Dan took one look at the tub full of water with steam rising from it and tried to put *his* foot down. He turned out to have amazing reserves of strength for an animal so skinny. When the washers and their subject emerged from the bathroom, the dog was clean but every square inch of the bathroom was wet. So were the washers. So were all the towels. And so on. Gretchen allowed as how it would have been easier for her to have done it herself. It sounded like trying to get Charlie to do certain chores.

Could the dog stay in the house? Of course not. Who knew whether he was housebroken? It turned out he was. Matthew opined that the old gentleman had too much dignity to make a mess in his living space, and after only a few days it was clear that the whole Corn House was Uncle Dan's living space.

But there was the matter of food. Not the dog's, the Lewises'. The following Sunday Gretchen put a cooked roast on the counter and went to the porch to ask Charlie's father to come and carve. By the time they reentered the kitchen, Uncle Dan had the roast on

the floor and had miraculously consumed half of it.
The dog looked up with not a trace of guilt on his face
and was in fact outraged when Mr. Lewis heaved him
out the door. A discussion ensued about whether to
eat what was left. In the end the remaining roast was
washed off and put in the refrigerator for sandwiches
and the Lewises had macaroni and cheese for Sunday
lunch. The logic of this compromise escaped everyone
but Gretchen. But from then on, food—particularly,
but not exclusively, meat—was never left alone with
Uncle Dan. It just never crossed his mind that it was
not fair game. And if you smacked him, his dignity
was affronted, and none of the Lewises could stand to
do that.

Uncle Dan showed no inclination to wander from
his newfound heaven. It was as if the old boy had suddenly grown roots right out of his splayed feet. He
would accompany Charlie to the barn but not on ex-
peditions around the farm with the pony. When Charlie started away in any direction, Uncle Dan would go
home to his place under the porch. His sailing days
were apparently over.

But on one occasion that October Uncle Dan
showed his real colors, his true vocation, the occupa-
tion of his youth. He and Charlie were crossing the
overgrown garden patch on the way to the barn. Uncle Dan was flopping along behind Charlie. There was
nothing out of the ordinary. It was just an October afternoon in Virginia. Then in an instant it all changed.
The dog floated forward two strides, fluidity and power

in his movement. He stopped and went rigid all over —with his nose held level and his possum tail straight behind him. It was an electrifying moment. Charlie later said he was so startled that for a second he was almost afraid. Something utterly new had entered his world. He knew what a pointer was, but he had never seen one do it before. The world slammed to a halt. There they were. Now what? The dog gave him no clue. Charlie had the feeling that he could have gone home and come back the next day and the dog would still have been there. Charlie felt the burden of action shift to him. He realized that the dog was waiting for him to do something. Charlie knew the birds were in front of him. But they were invisible. How could the dog have known? He never even put his nose to the ground . . .

Charlie walked forward a stride. He knew what was going to happen, knew that when the covey rose up it would be like an explosion, that the beating of the wings would feel almost physical, knew that when it happened, he would be as surprised as if he hadn't known the birds were there, even though he knew they were there. The dog didn't move until the quail flew. But when they were gone and there was nothing for him to retrieve, the dog turned to the boy with a look of disappointment, as if the boy had let him down. The covey was never again in his little territory, so Uncle Dan didn't point again that fall. He showed no interest in hunting for the birds.

• • •

CHARLIE WAS DETERMINED to hunt on his own. But fall was upon them and there was hunting with Luke and Sarah, so he didn't pursue hunting with bird dogs until the following spring. In the meantime Uncle Dan seemed to have found the fountain of youth. Everyone agreed that he had blossomed. He gained weight and his coat became shiny. The idea was even put forward that he had grown back some of the hair on his tail. Certainly many of his scars had filled in, or at least Gretchen thought so. He was an amiable presence at the Corn House. He greeted everyone with dignity and became in his own way a landmark. But even in his newfound youth, he showed no inclination to hunt. On the rare occasion when he walked up on a covey, he was dynamite, but he deviated not one inch from his route in search of the quarry that he had been bred for generations to find.

Charlie's idea was that he would go hunting on horseback—like the mounted foxhunters. Uncle Dan would be his pack. So one Saturday the following April, he saddled the pony and started up the hill behind the barn, calling Uncle Dan. The dog followed to the edge of the creek—the creek was a convenient place to get a drink on a warm day, so it was part of the old dog's territory. From the other side Charlie called. The dog looked at him with his tail swinging slowly back and forth and his head held low. Charlie —or, more accurately, the pony—took a step. The boy looked back and called again. This time in a more commanding tone of voice.

"Uncle Dan, come behind." He used this command because he had heard the huntsman say it to his pack when he was ready to move off somewhere. It had no visible effect on the dog except that he stopped wagging his tail. So there they were: Charlie on his side of the creek with the pony and Uncle Dan on the other, with the latter categorically refusing to move, no matter what tone of voice or actual words Charlie used. Uncle Dan's look was downright quizzical, as if he couldn't imagine what Charlie could possibly be asking of him. For Uncle Dan, Charlie's side of the creek just didn't exist.

"Then what did you do, Charlie?" asked Matthew in a serious tone. They were standing around in the store that evening. Everyone was smiling except Charlie.

"I went back across the creek and tried to chase him across the way the whips chase the hounds to the huntsman when he calls them."

"Well?" Matthew asked, still in his serious tone. "What happened?"

Here Charlie again became aggravated just thinking about it. "That old dog is stubborn as a mule. All we did was go around and around in a circle like a cat chasing her tail and the pony getting mad and me, too. And that dog looking at me like he couldn't imagine what I wanted him to do when I knew he knew perfectly well what I wanted him to do which was to follow me . . ." Charlie had to pause to catch his breath.

"But Charlie," said Jimmy Price, the kid from whom they had bought the pony, "you need a hound whip to make that old dog mind." Jimmy was an all-around aficionado when it came to horses and hunting.

Matthew turned to him sharply. "What you talking about a hound whip, Jimmy. That wouldn't do no good without a huntsman to chase the dog to . . ." He turned back to Charlie. "Anyway, if you going by yourself, you got to get the dog coming to you when you call. You need to see old man Jared Pugh. He's a bird-dog man, he'll know what to do."

The following afternoon after Sunday lunch, Charlie walked down to Jared Pugh's funny little house next to the depot. Charlie thought of it as a ginger-bread house because Mr. Pugh had built it himself over a number of years from various mismatched bricks and cinder blocks that he picked up at sales. It started out a cinder-block house. Then Mr. Pugh started adding bricks of many colors. It was a strange, multi-colored cottage just below the train depot. Behind it in the tiny back yard were two pens where Mr. Pugh kept his two bird dogs. Unlike the hounds who lived together, the bird dogs were kept separately.

Jared Pugh managed the depot. In those days the mail still left on the train in the morning and evening and freight was loaded and unloaded. Water from the spring next to the Corn House came a mile through a two-inch metal pipe to the depot. In the old days the water had supplied the steam locomotives that stopped to top off the tanks before they went through the cut in Burdens Mountain to the valley and then to

West Virginia. The steam locomotives were long gone
—there were diesel locomotives now. They lacked the
comforting sound of the big drivers on the steam en-
gines. When Charlie was eight his father had taken
him to the depot and arranged to have him go aboard
one of the huge, hissing locomotives while it was taking on water. The engineer had even let him ride in
the cab the hundred yards from the water pipe to the
depot building. Charlie's father in his most solemn
voice had made very clear to Charlie that he was wit-
nessing the end of a chapter in American history.
Charlie was wide-eyed when he described the heat
and noise of the engine's cab to Gretchen. He said
that the floor plates were so hot you couldn't have
gone barefoot in there even in winter, and the fireman
looked like a devil in a picture book what with all the
grime and coal dust streaking his overalls and the
heavy cloth cap almost covering his eyes stark white in
contrast to the coal blackness.

Jared Pugh and Charlie's father where waiting on
the platform when the engine arrived at the end of the
hundred-yard journey from the water pipe. Jared caught
Charlie's hands as he jumped and lowered him to the
heavy creosote-soaked boards of the platform. The locomotive hissed itself back into movement and started
westward to the long grade up the side of Burdens
Mountain. It was not the last steam locomotive to
stop at the depot for water, but it wasn't far from the
last one.

For once, Charlie was without words as he stood

between the two adults and watched the train slowly move away. Just watching the huge wheels make the steel track move up and down was a little frightening.

"How much longer before they start hauling the mail on trucks, Jared?" asked Charlie's father.

"Three, maybe four years, Mr. Lewis. I'm waiting for them to stop picking up freight any time now. Time's coming when the trains through here won't be hauling nothing but coal. Don't need a depot for coal trains."

Jared Pugh lived alone in his many-colored house with his two bird dogs. His wife had died years before from cancer and Jared, who had never been talkative, had gotten so quiet that except for the business of the depot he might not say ten words a day. He was a short, kind of pudgy man with thin red hair, big feet and long arms that hung out too far from his shirt sleeves and ended in large red hands that were amazingly precise for such an otherwise awkward sort of man.

CHARLIE WAS TENTATIVE about going to Mr. Pugh's house that Saturday. It wasn't that he was afraid of Jared, it was just that there had been little contact between the two—no thread to connect them, until now. Once Charlie got going it was fine. The thread was the bird dogs. Charlie explained his problem with Uncle Dan.

"He just won't come with me at all, Mr. Pugh. No matter what I do. I even tried some meat scraps to coax him, but he won't cross that creek. That dog is just totally lazy. What can I do?" By this time Charlie had worked himself up into a state, and Jared Pugh, no matter how quiet he was, couldn't help being amused at this blond boy all wound up about an old bird dog who wouldn't cross a creek to go hunting.

"You need another dog, Charlie. Maybe that would make your old dog come along, when he seen another one going." There was a long pause while Mr. Pugh looked first at the ground and then at Charlie as if making up his mind about something. Finally he looked up and said, so slowly that his mouth was actually open for a while before the words came out, "I need to go over to Mr. Winthrop's to pick up a dog he's giving me. I wasn't going till next week but I reckon I could go now if you want to come along." Here there was another long pause. "Just let me call over to his house to be sure he's home. Be right back."

Mr. Pugh emerged from his cottage in a few minutes, nodding his head yes. Charlie helped load the dog crate onto the pickup. The Winthrop's were rich and their farm was called an estate. It was a ten-mile drive, and because Mr. Pugh drove nearly as slow as he talked there was plenty of time for Charlie to get the story on the dog they were going to pick up.

His name was Donald and that's what everyone called him—Donald. Not Don or Donny, Donald. Donald was a champion field-trial English pointer. Mr. Winthrop had grown so fond of the dog that when his field-trial days were over, Donald came to live in the house with the Winthrops. The problem arose when Mickey—an asthmatic, and therefore evil-tempered, sixty-pound English bulldog, who was also Mr. Winthop's pride and joy and who also lived in the house—was introduced to Donald. Their hatred for one another was instant and implacable. After the first battle, it took the veterinarian close to an hour to sew the two of them back up. A plan was devised to introduce them to each other slowly but to no avail, and the second time the veterinarian had to sew them up, he suggested to Mr. Winthrop that this just wasn't going to work. In this second battle Mickey had gotten one of his ears split absolutely in half and to everyone's amusement, except Mr. Winthrop's, appeared to have three ears.

Because of Jimmy Price, not all of this story was new to Charlie. Jimmy, who shod the Winthrop horses, said that he thought that Mickey and Mr. Winthrop looked alike at least until the advent of the third ear. Then Mickey became something bizarre beyond imagining. As an illustration of Mickey's bad temper, Jimmy related the time Mr. Winthrop was driving his new Jeepster with the top down out the lane past the stable to get the paper with Mickey sitting majestically in the backseat. There were weeping willows hanging over the lane that had never been pruned and therefore hung down below the level of the windshield. As they passed under the trees, Mickey let out a growl of aggravation, reached up, and grabbed a mouthful of the branches before they could whip across his face.

And being a bulldog, he refused to let go. Mr. Winthrop glanced over his shoulder at the growl just in time to see Mickey snatched bodily from the Jeepster. Without another glance, Mr. Winthrop continued on his way, leaving Mickey's huge bulldog body bobbing up and down in the air in complete defiance of gravity, still growling in aggravation. Jimmy swore the dog hung in the air for a full minute, but nobody believed him. Finally Mickey let go, dropped squarely onto the driveway, and didn't move. On the way back Mr. Winthrop, who was nearly as jowly as Mickey, stopped the car and the two of them glared at each other. Finally Mr. Winthrop got out of the Jeepster, opened the passenger door, and beckoned to Mickey who grudgingly hopped back into the car because he was so lazy he wouldn't walk across the lawn to the front porch when he could ride, even if his dignity had been hurt. As the dog jumped into the car, Jimmy distinctly heard Mr. Winthrop say, "Well, I hope you learned something from that, you hardheaded bastard."

So it was easy to see why Donald really didn't have a chance in that world. He had spent his life going about the business of bird-dog field trials and living in a kennel by himself. So after the second war had resulted in the third ear for Mickey, Mr. Winthop had the good sense to call Jared.

The two of them, Mickey and Mr. Winthrop, were waiting at the kennel door when Charlie and Jared drove up. Charlie said later that he took one look at the bulldog and had to use all his manners and then some to keep from bursting out laughing. No story or description could have prepared him for what that dog looked like.

"Gretchen," he said to his mother, "that is the absolutely ugliest dog on earth. It's true what Jimmy said about him looking like he has three ears. And Mr. Winthrop and the bulldog do look alike, except for the three ears, of course . . ." At this point Charlie was overcome with laughter.

Gretchen tried to look stern. "You did mind your manners, didn't you, Charlie?"

"Yes ma'am, but it was hard with that thing snuffling away and wagging his funny tail. He's nice to people. He let me pat him. But his face is covered in slobber and those teeth stick out every which way . . . and Mr. Winthrop does talk through his nose just like the bulldog does." Realizing what he had just said, Charlie was further overcome with laughter. Gretchen smiled. She liked to see her often solemn boy laugh.

DONALD SEEMED PERFECTLY happy to jump into the dog crate and when they arrived at the cottage back at the depot his tail was waving and if dogs can smile, he was smiling. Mr. Pugh had arranged his tiny kennel so there was a third run. He had turned a barrel on its side so Donald would have a place to get into out of the weather. The two other pointers barked a greeting to Donald who went happily to the barrel and crawled into the straw bedding and lay down facing outward, at peace again with the world.

"Why does he like being in that little pen, Mr. Pugh? You'd think he'd hate being cooped up in that little space."

"He's ten year old, Charlie, and he's spent most of those years either in a little pen or hunting. Maybe he thinks that now he's in the pen he'll go hunting again. I guess it's all in what you're used to. I'll bring him up tomorrow afternoon and we'll see how he gets along with your dog. After messing with that bulldog, I hope he ain't gone sour on all dogs. God knows that bulldog don't look any other dog in creation, so maybe he thought he was fighting an entirely different kind of animal."

When Jared Pugh arrived the next afternoon, everyone was waiting. Charlie had Uncle Dan on a leash and his father and Gretchen were standing by in case of an emergency, although what the emergency might be was not at all clear. Mr. Pugh opened the crate door and clipped a lead on Donald's collar who jumped to the ground his tail wagging.

When Gretchen saw the still visible scars on Donald's neck she gasped. "Jared, that's awful. Did that bulldog really make all those scars?"

"Yes ma'am, he sure did. They tell me it took three men to pry him off this pointer, and when he let go, he was so mad he grabbed that boy what takes care of the stable on his arm, and it took the other two to get the dog off of *him*. That bulldog is tough."

Uncle Dan was invigorated. He raised his head and pulled his ears back and positively pranced over to

Donald. The two of them sniffed noses briefly but then sniffed each other's hind end to get the real message as to who each was. The hair on their backs went up and Gretchen put her hand to her mouth. Jared Pugh stood looking at the dogs, relaxed. Charlie watched the dogs with one eye and Mr. Pugh with the other in case trouble started. Everything was fine.

"Let's turn them loose, Charlie, and we'll see what your dog knows."

In the course of the introductions, Uncle Dan seemed to have become a different creature. When the leashes were removed, Jared blew a short note on the whistle he had on a cord around his neck. Both the dogs bounced over to him, their tails waving hard. They followed close as the procession moved across the barn lot. Mr. Pugh crossed the creek behind the barn on the stepping-stones. Still the dogs were right with him.

"Mr. Pugh, how did you do that? The only way I could get that dog across the creek would be to drag him."

What had happened was soon clear. The presence of the other dog and the knowing man with the whistle made the difference. Uncle Dan began to reconnect with his past.

"Come on up with me, Charlie, and you'll see what to do."

For the next hour Charlie concentrated with all his power as Jared Pugh took the bird dogs hunting. Charlie knew that Jared would have little to say and the only way to learn would be to watch and ask very few questions.

It was clear that Uncle Dan had been a field dog and that it had been a long time ago. After fifteen minutes Mr. Pugh said, "He's a hunting dog all right. But he don't remember exactly how to do it. See him watching Donald?"

Charlie saw. The first time the pointers came on point together Charlie shivered in spite of the heat. Most people say that the experience of flushing a covey—with its whirr of wings and the rising cloud of birds—is always new no matter how many times you've seen and heard it. This was certainly true for Charlie, who in the past had mainly flushed coveys by accident. Somehow the suspense was even greater if you knew what was about to happen because of the dogs.

Mr. Pugh quartered the big field, using the whistle and hand signals to have the dogs hunt where he wanted them to. The man and the two dogs were like a single creature. The dogs were like an extension of Jared Pugh's mind. He reached out over the fields through them and found the coveys. He paid special attention to the grown-up streambeds. Charlie could see why. The waterways provided both cover and water. The dogs naturally tended to hunt in grown-over areas where the quail would feel secure.

They found three coveys in an hour and a half. The fact that the farm was not really farmed anymore, that it had been let go, made it nearly perfect country for the bobwhite. The birds were there in abundance. Beginning early in the spring and throughout most of the summer the loud "bob white, bob bob white" call was incessant. By late spring of any year Charlie would have seen a hen cross one of the dusty lanes on the farm with her brood following along single file. Sometimes she would stop in the middle of an especially dusty lane and the whole brood would have a bath, creating a little dust cloud all around themselves in their enthusiasm.

THE SECOND TIME they went out, Jared Pugh let Charlie carry the whistle and work the dogs. Uncle Dan came right along and Donald followed Charlie's directions from the beginning. Mr. Pugh walked along behind smiling. The boy knew every inch of the fields and was already thinking like a quail.

When Charlie walked into the milking barn that evening, Matthew looked up with a question on his face. Charlie had the dreamy look he got sometimes when thinking back on something good.

"They were fine. Just fine," he said, answering Matthew's unspoken question. "They did just what I asked. We went together to find the birds and it all worked. Even with Mr. Pugh there, it was like being totally alone with the fields and the dogs and the birds." Here he looked up and smiled. "But it wasn't lonely. Each time I blew the whistle, they both looked back to see which way I wanted them to hunt. Mr.

Pugh says I can come and get Donald any time I want and that it's okay to go on the pony with them." He paused. "He says it's okay to go again tomorrow if I go over to the pond field and leave the birds behind the barn alone."

Charlie went for Donald early the next morning. When he returned, Uncle Dan fell right in. The two bird dogs waited patiently while Charlie saddled the pony. Charlie mounted. He blew a short note on the whistle and started up the hill toward the cattle guard with the two dogs right behind him. Halfway up he stopped the pony and looked back to be sure the dogs were still with him, that they were willing to follow the pony like they followed him on foot.

He would not go quail shooting with Jared Pugh in the fall. His mind was still on the hounds and the darker pursuit; but for now, in the late spring, he was happy with the pony and his dogs, who looked up at him with adoring eyes, waiting for him to blow the whistle to tell them where to hunt.

Gretchen had come to the porch door when Charlie blew the whistle. She smiled as she watched them start up the hill to the pond field—the nearly white pony and dogs and white-blond Charlie looking back over his shoulder at his dogs, excited about his new thing, his eyes shining.

Hog Killing

CHARLIE KNEW. You could see it in his eyes at Professor James's funeral, while Gretchen held on to his arm against his will. Gretchen didn't approve of funerals the way she didn't approve of death, but in this case she had no choice. Her slate-gray eyes were flat with grief, for she had come to love the old man. We could all see it. Sally had told it. From her we knew how Gretchen would sometimes on summer afternoons walk up the path to the big house to sit on the veranda and drink tea, which Sally served from the Victorian tea service that had belonged to the professor's mother. She listened to him talk about the past, sometimes about the curse left on the land by slavery, but also about the high days at Silver Hill when the world seemed to make sense and you could fool yourself in a minute into thinking that this little patch of ground was somehow exempt. That it was special—that love and respect and forbearance somehow made up for the fact that the colored children went to school in a one-room shack with a dirt yard. And how he believed that justice would one day prevail and the land would be healed, but not in his lifetime—all the same arguments as Mr. Jefferson, who had lived just on the other side of town and told himself the same story. We all knew it. You couldn't live in that part of the world and not know about Mr. Jefferson.

Once while he was talking, Sally happened to stop, coming out of the pantry and, as she told it later, "seen the look on Miz Lewis's face while she listened to Professor." With a smile on her slightly opened lips, as if the craggy-faced, seventy-four-year-old man with the wispy gray hair were giving her a gift or telling her a secret. Sally said—and here she fell into the speech of an older time—she had never seen Missy look so reposed and open and happy, and beautiful, what with her blond hair pulled back from her face in barrettes and her gray eyes shining. But then her face closed again, and she interrupted him in her tight voice.

"But in the meantime, what about Charlie? What will his story be? I've tried to make him understand that this is all passing. That he must find something else to love. But of course he won't listen to me." And her voice trailed off, nearly into tears.

The old man reached for her hand. And in the late summer silence of birds and insects, they sat. Then he looked at her. You could see what he was seeing; what old men see—the two of them together and how it would have been, and how they would have had children to come after him instead of their few moments together—and him nearing the end.

Then he spoke in an old man's voice, in a finished voice, "My love, Charlie tied himself to this ground. I don't know how it happened. It just did." Here he paused, and then in a low voice: "I am not called to know the future."

Two weeks later he died. It was the end of August.

There in the church, Charlie—with the same gray eyes as his mother's—glanced sideways at Matthew next to him in the pew. It was the first time that they had ever been in a church together. The races didn't go to church together then. You could see that Charlie wanted to reach over and hold on to Matthew's sleeve, as he always had done when he was little. But it was too late. Now he was fourteen and as tall as both Matthew and Gretchen, but with all the awkwardness of fourteen. Everything was changing, except his eyes.

The whole county was there at the Episcopal church in town, because the James family had lived in the area long before the Episcopal church in the village was even a mission. That is, everybody except Mrs. James, who was bedridden, lying in the big bedroom on the second floor, and Charlie's father who was away on business and couldn't get back in time.

Sally had stayed behind at Silver Hill preparing for the onslaught with three of her sisters to help, saying she didn't put stock in funerals nohow, while tears made rivers down her black face.

So the three of them were together as they filed past the casket in the parish house. Charlie had never seen a dead man before—lots of animals, including the mule—but never a person. Gretchen had seen her parents. Heaven knew how many dead people Matthew had seen and buried in the cemetery behind the colored church, which instead of a cross on its steeple had a carving in the shape of a clenched fist with the index finger pointing straight up. Some of us thought the finger was to direct our attention to God. Others thought it was the hand of rage pointing in accusation at the God of sorrows.

When they went to the pew to await the minister and the casket, Charlie was very pale. The three of them stood close to one another, Charlie in the middle. The priest came down the aisle followed by the casket. The words were said. Then it was over, and we were at the graveside with the late summer thunder, rain coming, and the minister saying in a half chant, "Unto Almighty God we commend the soul of our brother and we commit his body to the ground, ashes to ashes, dust to dust; in sure and certain hope of the resurrection . . ."

There were tears in Gretchen's eyes in spite of her anger at them, and they were now pouring down

Matthew's dark face. Charlie rocked back and forth a little, in cadence with the ancient language as if he knew it by heart.

The three of them stood close to the grave watching the men shovel in the red clay. All of us standing there were somehow drawn to look at them and not the grave—to look at the pale, adolescent white boy, standing between the black man and his mother, waiting for the rain.

THERE WAS A MOB at Silver Hill. The white people walked up the front brick path through the boxwoods, so thick on either side they almost touched. The storm door was still up from the winter. The screen door had somehow been overlooked the previous spring what with so much sickness in the house and Matthew and Sally feeling slow, knowing that everything was about to end. They had known it for a long time, but now, in that final spring season, somehow they were unable to stand up straight and be brisk and walk on.

Matthew and Sally had made their plans. Their new house across the railroad bridge was finished and neat. Matthew and Robert would do the odd jobs around the neighborhood—"custom work"—and Sally would go to work for Mrs. Buford, whose husband was a doctor at the university and lived on Owens Mountain, around from Luke and Jessie Henry.

Then the professor was gone, and there we all were, standing in the formal parlor in the old part of the house, brick, built even before the Declaration, when the land was frontier and tobacco land was cut out of the living woods by ringing the trees and planting the tobacco around the stumps and then, in four years, moving on. But the land was forgiving and generations of trees had come and gone, until finally the fully cleared pastures were completely grown up in broom sage and the fence lines choked with the cedars seeded by the birds sitting on the wire fences.

Mrs. James was in an old-fashioned wheelchair with a caned back and bottom, looking frail and nearly finished, which she was. She only lasted two months after they moved her to the nursing home in town. She had lived at Silver Hill for fifty years. Although she cared little for the outdoors or even gardening, she loved the old house with its added electricity and radiators and its creaky, wide-board floors, which if you went barefoot would stick you with a splinter if you weren't careful. The old kitchen where Sally still churned butter was unchanged since the twenties. It was only in the last five years that they had a refrigerator to take the place of the icebox, only ten years since the icebox was filled from the icehouse next to the garage, which in turn was filled every winter from the ice pond on the lower lane across from the rock, where Charlie had seen the wild dogs kill the doe.

In the dining room, the table and sideboard were laid out with white linen, long ago yellowed, and the silver all polished. Hams cured on the place were sliced paper thin and set on trays with new biscuits.

There was also potato salad surrounded by carrot sticks and sliced celery and sweet pickles. Vernon Maupin, Frank's brother, stood behind a side table at the end of the room, serving iced tea with lots of mint. And whiskey, too, to them that wanted it.

The kitchen was full of colored people who had come in the screened porch door into the back pantry. Charlie, from custom, had walked around to the back, leaving Gretchen to go up the front walk alone. She had started to say something, but thought better of it. He walked into the kitchen, where his pale skin and nearly white hair were set off in contrast to the black faces. He was more than five and a half feet tall, on the level with most adults. In the kitchen there was age and grief and change. Charlie was the youngest in the room, by a lot.

"Reckon we better plan right now for hog killin,'" said Billy Abel, almost in a whisper. "The way things be, who knows, it might not happen this year. Or maybe ever again."

"Go on with you, Billy! What you mean? Just because Professor gone don't mean everything going to change," said Sally's sister, Jean—because Billy always thought things would work out bad, no matter what.

Then Charlie in his loud voice said, "No need to wait. It's all changed already!" He was looking around at the kitchen as if this would be the last time he ever saw it, which it was.

Fred Henry spoke up in his talky way, "What's

wrong, Charlie? Don't you like living in your new house? I know your mama and daddy glad to be out of the Corn House, what with it so small, and all . . ." Uncharacteristically, he stopped. Everyone knew how Charlie felt about leaving the Corn House and moving to the big house across the tracks on the other side of the village. You could see it in his eyes when he got off the bus in the village instead of riding on up the hill to the lane at Silver Hill. In spite of knowing the village like the back of his hand, having grown up in it, he would look around like he was lost or in the wrong place. Then he would turn away and trudge up the bank and across the railroad and onto the lower lawn of his new home.

A ways down the hall to the dining room, Robert Paine said to Billy, "It don't matter whether hog killing goes or not for Charlie. He been baptized in that branch once—and that's enough for anybody, even Charlie." He looked up to be sure Charlie had heard. Charlie was used to the tension between them. It had always been there.

BUT IT WAS TRUE. Charlie had surely been immersed in that branch. It had happened five years ago, when he was nine. Before that, Charlie had just been around. Almost like any other kid. Everyone in the community knew him, because he looked so different. But at that hog killing things changed. And all because the pipes burst at the school one night in the January cold snap. It took ten days to fix the pipes, and it happened that hog killing went on during that time. So after Gretchen's fears had been calmed by the professor, Charlie got to go along with Matthew, as he and Robert went around the neighborhood picking up the slaughtered hogs.

Hog killing took place each year just after a hard freeze in January. Billy and Matthew would meet up in the store one morning.

"Reckon it's time, Matthew?" It was both a question and a statement.

"Reckon so, Billy . . . Monday?"

Word would go around the neighborhood, and Monday morning it began. Everyone in the area kept hogs. Some had one, some five. They were usually kept in plain board pens down the hill behind each house. They stank and squealed and ate garbage and feed from the co-op. On the appointed day, the men in the family went down to the pen with the .22 and the long, razor-sharp butcher knife.

By the time Matthew and Robert arrived, the hogs were supposed to be dead and bled out. But if there weren't men in the family or the shooter had missed, Matthew and Robert would help out and get the job done. They would return to the village with five hogs at a time, a truckload, each with an ear notched in a special way so the men could keep track of the owners.

Behind the store, next to the branch, there was a huge metal scalding tub with a fire under it. The hogs were loaded into it one at a time. Billy Abel, who had blue eyes in his dark face and was a man of many words, wore a ridiculously tall chef's hat to preside over this ritual. He looked like a cross between a witch and a clown, brandishing his butcher knife as he danced around giving orders with the steam rising all about him from the scalding tub. His first job was to delicately test the water with his index finger while being careful not to slip down the frozen bank into the branch. Standing next to him by the tub would be James Walker, who was six foot five. He held a bucket of cold water from the branch ready to pour a little in each time Billy hollered that the water was getting too damn hot. The water had to be just the right temperature for the hogs to let go of their hair, so that Matthew and Robert and Leonard could shave each one with the razorlike knives after it had been heaved up to the edge of the tub. That done, two other Walker brothers would lift the hog out of the tub and hang him up by the hind legs on the racks set up next to the road. Everyone had to be careful about slipping. The ground was frozen solid, but as the day went on, the surface became slick with blood and thawed ice.

When there were five hogs hung up, Billy would, with another flourish, zip his knife down the belly of each one. As the guts cascaded out, they were caught in large pans to be separated out for sausage and scrapple. They kept most except the lungs—the men called them "lights"—which were slung up into the air by the windpipes and caught on the power lines running along the road. In that way everyone who drove by could tell how the hog killing was going by the number of lungs hanging from the wires.

To a stranger, it would have looked like something from another world, certainly not like the end of the forties in America what with ten black men talking and laughing as they heaved the huge hog carcasses around in the steamy mist with the lights and windpipes hanging overhead on the wires, and Billy doing his dance, with his knife and his chef's hat, talking his head off, his blue eyes flashing with pleasure.

Charlie loved it, from the first second. He was like a blond ghost dodging in and out, asking questions so fast that not even Billy could keep up with answers. "Why do you scrape that thick, old hair off the hogs, Billy?"

"Well, Charlie, sometimes we cook the pork with the skin on. Wouldn't do to have that thick, old, bristly hair on our plate, would it?"

On and on during the morning. Until about the fifth hog, hanging on to Matthew's coat while he was scraping a hog, Charlie said in a dreamy voice, "Matthew, how many years have you been doing this?"

Then just slick as you please, Charlie slipped right down the icy bank into the branch, which was two and a half feet deep.

Robert Paine hollered, "Look out! God damn it! I told you Matthew not to let that little white boy in here."

Charlie let out a yell as he struck the cold water, slid on the muddy bottom, and for a second disappeared completely from sight.

There was total confusion. Billy, still the comic demon, leapt up and down, waving his butcher knife and hollering, "Oh my God! Miz Lewis going to kill us! Oh my God! What we going to do, Matthew? That boy going to drown!" while Matthew, as usual, took charge of the situation and put a handy fence board across the branch—which was really just a ditch about four feet wide. But it *was* over two feet deep. By the time Charlie surfaced, the whole crew had gathered around on both sides of the branch.

Charlie could swim. His daddy had taught him in the pond behind Silver Hill when he was seven. But he'd never been in cold water like that. So he let out with another mighty yelp as he reared up from the water covered with mud and ice, then slipped and fell back in again.

Matthew was yelling, "Grab the board, Charlie! Grab the damn board!"

On the second try, Charlie grabbed the board and hung on like death as Matthew clutched at him from one side of the branch and Leonard from the other. The problem was that they each got an arm and pulled. And for a second it looked like all three would end up back in the branch, which would have struck a tremendous blow to everyone's dignity. There would be laughter in the store for at least the next ten years.

"Let go, Leonard!" Matthew bellowed and heaved at Charlie's coat sleeve, almost pulling the coat ashore and leaving the boy behind. But Charlie somehow stayed inside the coat and ended up in Matthew's arms, already shivering uncontrollably.

As Mr. Dudley opened the back window of the post office to see what the yelling was all about, he saw a cluster of black men peering into the branch next to the scalding tub, as if they had added some new twist to the normal ceremony of hog killing. But it was just Charlie, and since the phrase "just Charlie" was already becoming a staple in the talk of the village, no one was one really surprised when Matthew rushed into the store, nearly carrying Charlie, and set him down on the nail keg next to Aunt Millie Mays's old rocking chair.

Aunt Millie was a very old black lady with only two bottom teeth, who spent her days in the winter sitting next to the pot belly in the store. For many people, she was a mystery. Some people weren't even sure who she was or where she had come from. But in winter, she was always there. Watching. Staring at people. Never saying anything. That day she took one look at Charlie and began to cackle in a high, crazy old voice —pointing and gabbling, "You done took a bath now, Charlie Lewis, for sure. That's just what you need— washing in all that hog blood and mud and water. Now you know what it's like . . ." She paused to draw breath, and then began again, with real urgency, "Where you come from, Charlie Lewis? Where? Tell me where?" Rocking and cackling, holding on to her head scarf with one hand and pointing with the other forefinger, which was almost bent double with arthritis, at Charlie who looked up at her, startled, for a second. Almost afraid.

People didn't usually pay Aunt Millie any mind. But something in her crazy voice made everyone in the store stop now and stare at Charlie.

He was just a skinny, nine-year-old boy, with his mother's fair coloring. He was just Charlie, huddled there in his winter coat, having been washed in that branch sure enough, even though by mistake, but soaking wet, nonetheless, and to whom Aunt Millie never spoke another word.

Then the spell was broken and Matthew was cranking the phone and telling the operator he wanted number 32. Gretchen came on the line and Matthew told her what had happened, and she was no doubt out the door before Matthew could hang up. She rolled into the gravel parking lot in a hurry, rushed into the store prepared to be furious—took one look at the bedraggled boy, sat down on the nail keg next to him, and clutched him in her arms, crooning, "Why do you do these things, Charlie? Why?" Always the same words.

Most of us thought she knew the answer, that it lay not very deep within herself but that for some reason she could not bring herself to speak it.

Hog killing went on and two hours later he was back, as he was each year following. Some years Charlie didn't see much of it because of school. But some years, if there was snow, he would be around for the whole thing. And every once in a while someone told the story again of Charlie being baptized in the branch and of Aunt Millie's pointing at him in the store and being so crazy. And everyone would laugh—Charlie, too—except Robert, who only laughed at his own jokes.

ON THIS FUNERAL DAY in the hall at Silver Hill, Robert laughed. He remembered it as his own story.

But Billy didn't laugh. He said to no one in particular, "Well, I'm asking around to see who's got hogs. Seems like not as many hogs around this year as usual . . ."

Just at that moment Alice Wilson, an old black lady who had been the maid at Silver Hill before Matthew and Sally came and was helping serve, called down the hall, "Charlie Lewis, your mama want you in this parlor right now to make your manners. And she say this instant! So you better come!" Charlie headed for the parlor right then because Alice could actually scare a person, even as gray and dried up as she was.

Alice's own famous story was about the time a poor old classmate of the professor's, who had become an alcoholic and ruined his life, kept coming around pan-handling until Alice had had enough. She warned the man that there would be trouble if he came around again. And sure enough, the next time he walked up the brick walk between the boxwoods, she came to the door with the professor's double-barrel 16-gauge and told him to get out of there, right now. The poor man then made the mistake of saying something about not having to take that kind of talk from a colored person, at which point she started counting to ten. He suddenly realized then that this old lady was serious and he started to run. But it was too late, because when she got to ten, she let go with one barrel of number 12 bird shot and blew the poor man the rest of the way down the brick walk. The village laughed about it for days. That would teach some old drifter, no matter who he was, to mess with Alice Wilson. There was all sorts of trouble with the law, but the professor took care of it. The story even had a happy ending because the man's people came and got him, and he went home and never had another drink for the rest of his life, at least so we were told.

But now Alice looked so bent over with age and grief you wouldn't have thought anything of her, until you looked into her fierce unyielding eyes as she took Charlie's arm to hurry him up to the parlor, and whispered, "Charlie you be a brave boy now. You hear me? Be brave!" And when he didn't turn his head, she jerked his arm. "Look at me, Charlie Lewis. Did you hear me?" And this time he did look into her almost black eyes and then down at her hand on his arm. A hand whose veins seemed as big as the bones, and said, "Yes ma'am, I hear."

Just as they entered the room, a tall white-haired man pushed past them on the way to the dining room.

"Who was that?" whispered Charlie.

"Oh, that's some big man from Richmond the

professor knowed for years." And here a small devilish smile came on her face, and she whispered, "Don't he just look walkingstickyfied? I swear I never did like that man." She pulled Charlie on into the parlor where Gretchen and Mrs. James were waiting.

Gretchen had made most of the funeral arrangements. There had been no one else, really, so she just stepped in and did it. Now she met Charlie's gaze coolly. She was standing next to Mrs. James, tall and erect and grim in her black dress, her hair pulled back in a bun at the base of her neck. Her posture said that she would do this bitter thing, no matter what. Charlie, if he had thought about it, would have understood the price she paid for her icy control. There must have been two hundred people in and around the house, all told. As each person came by to pay his or her respects, Gretchen, if she knew the name, would lean down and whisper to Mrs. James who it was. No one knew how much the old lady understood about what was going on around her. Sometimes she would act as if she knew nothing all.

As Charlie approached, she looked up sharply. She couldn't help but recognize him, and the right words just flowed out of her from her upbringing and all the many years of funerals. "Oh, Charlie, I'm glad to see you. But it is such a sad occasion. The professor would be so pleased that you are here to help your mother at this time."

Then suddenly her voice was hard-edged and rational, not the voice of a dying septuagenarian at all.

"But now what will you do, Charlie? There will be no one here. The professor gone. Matthew and Sally, and me . . . gone. You moved. Will you still ride around the farm? Or have you left here for good, too?"

Then silence. His mother caught Charlie's gaze, as if the question had been framed by her, or at least by the two of them, to put him to the test. For the moment the adolescent vanished and was replaced with the surety of Charlie's childhood. He pulled his shoulders back and said to Mrs. James, and to his mother, too, "I'll never leave here."

"Are you so sure, Charlie?" replied the old lady, softly. But then she changed back. "Well, be a help to your mama." She turned her gaze aside.

Charlie turned also and shuffled back down the hall to the kitchen where in the pantry Matthew was talking to the lawyer about the future, and the professor's will and Mrs. James.

"We need a timetable for when things will happen, Matthew. But we surely don't have one. As you know, the university inherits the farm, but I'm not clear when they will take it over, so you need to plan to stay on and keep things under control here until the final plans are made. And heaven knows when that will be. I even heard a rumor that the university doesn't want the place, what with the upkeep and so on. You and Sally will be paid as usual. Is that all right?" There was a note of urgency, and Charlie stopped. Matthew nodded yes, and the lawyer came past Charlie and went into the dining room.

Matthew and Charlie stood five feet apart in the hall with its old beaded wainscoting and peeling wallpaper. They were the same height and looked at each other on the level. Suddenly the dam broke for Charlie, and he was clutching Matthew, tears pouring from his eyes. He sobbed like a little boy, as Matthew patted him on the back with his huge, hard hand, crooning, "Now Charlie," over and over, as if the repetition of the name would have the same settling effect that it had when Charlie was a little boy. But now it was somehow different. Maybe it was too late for tears.

By October, Silver Hill was as empty as the Corn House. The university sent a crew out twice a week to maintain the place. The village said it would never work; that empty, the farm would go to wrack and ruin. The university leased out the big field behind the Corn House to a man who wanted to cross a Brahma bull on Angus cows. His idea was that the offspring would be tough and not need a lot of care. The man had stretched two strands of barbed wire around the whole 150 acres and brought in a huge Brahma bull and thirty Angus cows. After the bull and cows arrived, the man came to the store and told Mr. Dudley to warn everyone that that bull was mean and dangerous if you riled him up, but fine if you left him alone. Within two days half the village had trudged up the lane to the Corn House to try to catch a glimpse of the bull. Those who did brought back a description of an animal you might see in a zoo. His hump was said to stick up three feet over his back. He had little mean eyes. And thick horns. And so on.

This was, of course, enough for Charlie, who hadn't set foot on the place since the day of the funeral. He didn't take the pony. Instead, he took the chestnut ex-army horse a friend had given the Lewises with the vague idea that Mr. Lewis might like to ride. The pony and the horse stayed in the pasture behind the barn at Pine Hill and sometimes they would go a whole week seeing nobody. The problem with the army horse was that you had to be very careful with the reins, because if that horse got the bit in his teeth you had just as well pull on a telephone pole as try to stop him. He would jump anything.

The afternoon after he heard about the bull, Charlie caught the army horse, rode across the railroad track down the hill, crossed the highway, and passed the store just as Mr. Dudley came out to lower the flag.

"Going back to ride around your old place, are you, Charlie?" he asked.

"Yes sir, " Charlie replied. "I want to take a look at that bull."

"Better be careful. You've heard about him, haven't you?"

"Yes sir, I'll be careful."

Later Mr. Dudley said that he had wondered about the wisdom of that trip. He knew all about the army horse's habits. But Charlie was fourteen and had been riding around alone since he was eight, so Mr. Dudley thought no more about it.

Five o'clock came and people began pulling into the store on the way home. Matthew and Robert were inside getting a Pepsi when Mr. Dudley let out a holler and everyone rushed to the door to see the army horse running wide open on the way home without Charlie. The horse was whinnying in the hysterical way horses do when they think they're lost because they don't have a rider and the reins are flapping and the stirrups are banging on their sides. By a miracle the horse made it across the highway without being hit by a car or truck. Mr. Dudley told Matthew and Robert about Charlie going to see the bull, and they were out the door on the way to the Corn House before he stopped talking.

They found him in the middle of the road at its intersection with the lane to the Corn House. He was half awake, leaning on his hands, but sitting up. Blood was running down his face from a scalp wound. He looked up at Matthew and smiled.

"Hi."

Matthew was so furious he told us that he thought he would explode. He just couldn't believe that Charlie had done one of his things again. Or that there were any of his things left to do. Matthew used little profanity in his life, but if a count had been kept, a significant part of it would have to be given over to Charlie.

"Charlie, what in the name of God have you done to yourself this time!" Matthew's words came out in a torrent. There was fear, too. What if the kid had fractured his skull?

Robert was chuckling. "Better move him off the road, Matthew, before someone come along and runs us all over."

So they picked him up and put him in the backseat of Matthew's '36 Ford sedan on some feed sacks. They stopped at the store to tell Mr. Dudley they had found Charlie and that he would probably be all right.

Gretchen arrived at home to see Matthew's car in the back driveway. She had a sudden premonition and rushed into the house to find Charlie on the couch in the living room on a feed sack to keep from ruining the slipcover. He had stopped bleeding and was wide awake and telling his story. Gretchen didn't interrupt. She stood in the door and listened. But her face was stark white. The boy was a mess. With blood all over his front from the scalp wound.

Charlie, as was his habit, told the story with his old urgency to Matthew—not his mother. "I opened the gap the man made behind our barn. It was two boards tied to steel posts with bale string. I tied them back pretty low so if I needed to get out of there in a hurry, I wouldn't have any trouble jumping it. I found the herd right at the top of the hill. Matthew, you wouldn't believe that bull . . ."

Here Matthew looked as if he were going to interrupt, but seemed to think better of it, and Charlie continued.

"He looks twice as big as one of the cows. And he has tiny eyes. He looked up at me and didn't move. Like he was expecting me, or something. Then he did that moaning they do and pulled some dirt back with a front foot and flipped it over his back. I tell you that bull scared me."

Gretchen broke in, "At least you had that much sense!" which was so unusual that Charlie and the two men glanced at her. She was completely cool.

"Well anyway, the horse snorted, and I thought I'd better get out of there right then. But I didn't gallop, I trotted back toward the gap so the damn horse wouldn't get away from me. Well, anyway, as soon as I turned the horse, the bull came after me. And by the time we got to the gap, that bull was serious—Matthew, he is huge! So I jumped the gap and looked back over my shoulder to be sure the bull didn't jump, too. Well, he didn't, but while I was looking back, the horse got the bit and was gone. I mean, he ran *away* with me. There wasn't anything I could do except bail out, and I was scared to do that. So when he got to the hard road I was still with him. He turned sharp left, his feet went out from under him, and down we went. And smacked my head on the road. I guess it knocked me out. The next thing I remember is you and Robert and feeling the blood running down my face—"

That was enough for Gretchen. Matthew said he had never seen her so angry—and flushed now, where she had been pale before. "Go out and get in the car, Charlie. And take that feed sack with you so you don't bleed all over the seats."

There was no question about her tone of voice. Charlie went.

"Will you take care of the horse, Matthew? Just catch him and get the tack off and turn him out. I'll worry about him later."

So off they went to the emergency room. Charlie had a concussion and would have to stay in bed for two days, but the wound was just a scalp wound. The doctor said it was amazing that Charlie could remember what had happened considering the blow to the head he got. We laughed when we heard that idea, because Charlie would have kept that story in his head come hell or high water—just so he could tell it to Matthew and upset his mother.

Still, even after he recovered from his bull adventure, he looked pretty grim. A little like after the mule died. Or just after the funeral. Like he was grieving. We didn't know how he acted at school, but around the village, he just looked sad.

FALL PASSED, and in January there was a hard freeze, the time of wood smoke, and crows calling in the distance. And in spite of Billy's forebodings, hog killing went on. There were lots of hogs. On the appointed Monday, the steam rose again from the scalding tub, Billy did his dance, and the lights and windpipes were thrown across the wires as always. Monday and Tuesday morning Charlie saw the steam rising. He got on the bus as usual. Tuesday evening, just as it was getting dark, he went to the store for Gretchen. The men had finished for the day and were sitting on stump ends around a fire they had built.

They were in a close circle around the fire. Charlie slipped into the circle without a sound and sat down next to Matthew. There was a jug going around and it had stopped with Robert who took a long pull just as Charlie arrived. Then Robert hunched forward as if to ward off the cold, the jug dangling in one hand between his legs, head down.

No one said a word. Then, without lifting his head, he swung it to his left to look at Charlie. The way he swung his head you could tell he was drunk. And suddenly he was off the stump and slumped in front of Charlie, leaning on his arms. His face got closer and closer, until Charlie must have felt the heat of his breath and smelled the whiskey. The circle froze, everyone staring, waiting to see what Robert would do, knowing that the time had finally come. Charlie tried to look toward Matthew, but he was somehow unable to pull his eyes away from Robert, whose face in shadow was featureless and menacing. It was as if everyone had stopped breathing—waiting. Then right into Charlie's face, but speaking to Matthew, he said, "I done told you for years not to let the little white son of a bitch come around us. But you never would listen . . . Well, it don't matter now. He's gone. He just done growed out of us. Another year we won't see him no more . . . He may be sitting here now, but he gone sure enough. Gone at last. At last!" He laughed his choppy laugh and raised his left arm.

Matthew's huge hand shot out and gripped the

skinny arm. In his quiet voice, he said, "No more, Robert. You done said enough."

And for an instant, silence. And then Robert wobbled once and slumped forward right into Charlie's lap. Charlie jumped up, horror on his face, leaving Robert passed out on the ground. Then he turned and started toward the store.

"Charlie!" called Matthew. "Charlie!"

But the boy kept walking. In the iron January night, with a breeze springing up from the north, maybe bringing snow—too cold for hounds to run tonight—walking back toward the store, away from hog killing and the branch where he had been baptized. Walking up the hill, the other way, across the railroad.

And Matthew didn't call again.

C O D A

Circles

I HAVE NO MEMORY of why I was in the creek behind our barn that Sunday morning, barefoot. I guess I just found myself there. I do know about the barefoot part, though. I didn't wear shoes during the summer, except to church, or at least I didn't until I was fourteen and we had left the Corn House and the farm for good. I was twelve that Sunday morning and it was May. School would be out soon and summer starting, everything blooming, everything alive and chirping, or cooing or buzzing. Even the pony, looking over the fence at me, dozing in the late spring warmth, shone gray and fat after the winter's red mud and short grass.

So I was in the creek barefoot when I stepped on him. I say "him." I don't know which sex, really. But there was one damn sure thing—that snake was not an "it." He was three circles buried in the mud and water grass of the pool. He was still thin from the long winter. His backbone protruded above his body, and the skin was loose and moving as I pulled my foot away when the circles stirred under my weight—the way a snake does when you step on him. Not in fear exactly. I was startled. That's all.

I grabbed hold of a willow branch and pulled myself out of the creek and, glancing over my shoulder, went through the back door of the barn. There was an old rusty bucket hanging on the wall with the pitchfork next to it. Finding him a second time turned out to be a job. Finally I just waded around some more until I stepped on him again. Then I carefully slid the fork under the water to pick him up. He came up out of the water ready to travel, flowing over the tines like quicksilver, insubstantial, but there nonetheless. But not for long unless I did something quick. Just as he was about to drop off the fork, I had the bucket ready and in he went. He didn't try to escape; he coiled up again, making his circles in the bottom of the bucket as I watched. He looked just like any other snake to me. Not black, but almost black. No rattlesnake or copperhead markings. Just an almost-black snake. I hadn't been taught about pit vipers and diamond-shaped heads. It had just never come up.

But I was interested, so off I went to the house. It must have looked like a Norman Rockwell painting—the spring morning with honeysuckle and multiflora rose coming to bloom, the pony looking over the fence, and the kid in blue jeans, no shoes, and a hand-me-down white shirt, carrying a bucket, which the casual observer would have thought contained worms for a fishing expedition. The Sunday morning voices on the porch—domestic and secure—carried even as far as the creek behind the barn.

The ground-level screened-in porch was at the front of the house, which itself had been built for storing corn from the days when the farm was a real farm. When my father made the arrangement with Professor James to convert the building into a real house, there was no plumbing and no electricity. During the course of the first six months we lived there, my father installed a drain field, piped water from the spring-house, wired the place, painted it, built a bathroom and a kitchen. He decorated the kitchen with drawings in the Pennsylvania Dutch style called Peter Hunt. The resulting cottage was acknowledged by everyone to be a little "gem," in Gretchen's phrase.

So we found ourselves dug deep in the central Virginia countryside. Toward the end of her life, Gretchen once asked me if I remembered why we had come to Virginia in the first place. But I couldn't, and she, typically, got irritated at me for not knowing. How was I to know? I had been six when it happened. I do know that my father was in the worst of the Pacific invasions as a lieutenant on that 150-foot gunboat, was decorated, and only spoke once of what had happened beyond the mere facts. So there we were—two city parents and me, a kid absolutely ready for the whole experience.

My father remains a shadow. As I said, he did the Corn House with his own hands, as he did the remodeling of our second house. He stopped the wild-fire and saved a lot of people from ruin. He liked the countryside, but he never became part of it. He felt compelled to be involved with manufacturing as an executive and that forced him to spend much of his time away from home. There was no manufacturing around us then. After all, our country was Mr. Jefferson's country. But that was changing, too.

The church was my father's thing, that and two or three deep friendships—and ideas. He had ideas about the way things should be, which he expressed with vehemence that increased as the amount of drink he had taken in increased. Usually the ideas were perfectly sensible, but his opinionated way of telling them put people off.

At the appropriate time in my life, we fought like mad, but his memory has turned soft and the ideas of his I remember are gentle and understanding. Like the time when I was sixteen, in love and jilted, he took me up to one of the overlooks in the mountains, parked the car, and as we looked at the spectacular view of our home countryside, told me very quietly that he understood my pain. He said that the pain was real and that the soupy popular song that went, "They tried to tell us we're too young," was true, that love at sixteen, puppy love, was among the strongest of all human emotions. He said that I would get over it, but for now it just hurt. And even though he was imparting one of his ideas, it is a memory sweet beyond telling.

Now when I look at the age spots on my hands, I see his hands. He was dark. I remember his face in shadow. I have his same hooked nose. He was a churchman. In the early years, many mornings he served at the altar when there were just the angels, the archangels, the rector, his housekeeper, and my father in the church.

Of his friends, William Archer, the rector of the Episcopal church in the village, was the closest. Father Will—which is what I called him before I started calling him Uncle Will, much to everyone's amazement—was from an old New England private school family. His father had been the famous Episcopal priest headmaster of a famous Episcopal boy's prep school that for generations had pumped out Ivy Leaguers who then became, as used to be said, captains of industry and government, especially foreign affairs. This career, particularly the State Department part, had been decreed for Will from an early age, with becoming a "school man" a distant second. As hardheaded in his way as his father, Will opted for the school part. He got as far as becoming a priest. And then to his father's great displeasure, after seminary (where he soaked up C. S. Lewis, T. S. Eliot, and the Oxford movement and became an Anglo-Catholic), he ended up as a missionary to the people of the Blue Ridge Mountains. He was remarkably successful in this for one so sophisticated and urbane. One of the reasons was was that the men and boys of each mission became servers. Will was a near genius at making men and boys feel the drama of the Eucharist and that they were playing a vital role in this calling down of God to a specific place and moment. Somehow he got his people to make a leap beyond the preaching tradition they were familiar with, into the world of the Anglican Mass.

Sometimes it took hold in curious ways. There was a sheriff in one of the mountain counties who made the sign of the cross before he ate lunch in the single restaurant in his county seat, much to the horror of the natives, although they would have been hard put to say why the sign of the cross shocked them. But people got used to even this.

After fifteen years on the circuit, the mission church in our village became a parish and Will was called to be rector. He never left. As was his custom, he persuaded the boys and some of the men to become servers.

At some point in Will's life there had been a great love. I never knew the whole story, just that she had been in one of the girls' colleges of New England while Will was at Yale. Whatever happened, he remained a bachelor for the rest of his life. He was a tall, skinny man. Really skinny. The first time you saw him, you thought he must be dying of something. If so, it took thirty-eight years from my first memory of him for it to happen. The way he stood, usually with a cigarette in his hand and one hip cocked, exuded irony. Or maybe I mean humor—with a smile, but the kind of smile that overlays sorrow, like the loss of his love or the mornings at the altar when nothing happened and God was so distant you could barely see him, even in your praying eye.

It became his habit to come to our house for a drink after church and sometimes he stayed for lunch. At the time, the fashion was martinis, which my father mixed with great panache. It makes my stomach shrivel to think of those drinks. Even then they both drank too much.

They were like brothers in the struggle for faith, a struggle that never left either of them and that they passed on to me. Once when Charles and Gretchen were going on a trip, I became Will's godson by virtue of a paper Gretchen made him sign saying that if anything happened to them Will would raise me and that provisions had been made, etc., etc. The thought of suddenly inheriting a twelve-year-old, let alone me, made Will blanch, and me smile.

So THOSE ARE the characters and the scene. One more thing, though. For those of you—as I was —not in a sufficient state of grace to know what "cottonmouth" means, it refers to the dramatically white membranes on the inside of the water moccasin's mouth in contrast to his dark body. The cottonmouth has little holes on the side of his head that are called pits—hence, a pit viper. He is very poisonous but not particularly bad-tempered if let alone.

The screen door had an old-fashioned spring-loaded stop on it that made a clunk as I opened it. The snake made one of his regular strikes at my hand just as the three of them looked up at the sound of the door.

"Where the hell did you get that goddamn snake, Charlie?" yelled—I mean really *yelled*—my father.

Gretchen screamed and Will jumped up, spilling his fragile martini. By that time Daddy had crossed the intervening fifteen feet, knocked the bucket from my hand, knocking me down in the same motion, fortunately not where the snake fell. The bucket landed on its side, of course, and the next instant we had a three-and-a-half-foot cottonmouth moccasin flowing around the enclosed ten-by-seventeen-foot porch, looking for a way out where there was none, herding the people in front of him. That is, all except my father who had hotfooted it out of there to the outhouse, which had been converted to a toolshed, to get some implement to kill—not maim, *kill*—this creature that had intruded on our tranquil Sunday world.

He came back with a hoe. He was going to hoe the snake's head off. Have you ever tried to hoe the head off a snake in the open, that is, where the snake has freedom of movement? It's almost impossible, especially if there is porch furniture in the way. By this time Gretchen and Will were watching the proceedings from the safety of the kitchen, looking out over the Dutch door. But I was still out on the porch, also in the way.

So there we were. If this was the biblical struggle with evil, it had strong overtones of farce. Will, who had completely recovered his humor and was smiling broadly, spoke up. "Charles, it appears to me that if you succeed in killing this snake you no doubt will also make a mess of the furniture, not to mention the drinks. So in order to simplify the situation, why don't you get a big shovel and shovel him out the door, and he will crawl back to the branch and halfway to the village before he stops for breath, if snakes breathe." He was about to burst into laughter.

Up to this point, I was inclined toward killing, but at this speech, I converted and became vehement for clemency. Daddy wasn't sure. He was still very frightened for my sake. But after a pause, when Gretchen said, "Oh, Charles, just get the creature out of here," that is what we did. A scoop was gotten from the toolshed and the snake cajoled into sliding across the high sill of the screen door. He went fast down hill toward the weeping willow in the front yard. As he crossed one of the willow's big roots, a curious thing happened. In order to avoid a knob on the next root, he crawled back over himself, creating his last circle, I thought, for me. And he stopped for an instant, looking—if a snake looks—back toward us, all of us still full of the chill a snake brings with him. Then without a thought to the consequences, I blurted out, "That's how I found him. I was walking in the creek. I felt him move under my foot. He was in circles like that. That's all. I wasn't sure which kind he was . . ." I trailed off to nothing, waiting for the lecture.

Instead, Will looked straight at me and asked, "Do you want to learn to serve at the altar, Charlie?" I caught my breath. Sometimes twelve-year-olds were allowed to light the candles and carry torches, but never serve at the altar. I wasn't even confirmed.

But I had been closely watching Will and my father together at the altar in the early mornings, and I had heard the language of Cranmer and the King James Bible. And although the surface meaning of the words often escaped me, even then, I could hear the struggle toward God. I knew that beyond the farm and nature and the animals and Matthew and the other people I knew and loved, this was the center of their lives, and wondered without words whether it would become mine.

I already knew the danger of it. I'd felt the heaviness left sometimes after the last Gospel—after the words of St. John are repeated ("And the Word was made flesh and dwelt among us . . . full of grace and truth") and the response ("Thanks be to God)"—when my father walked from the church in front of Will, and I somehow knew that nothing had happened for him. I also knew that in that moment, at least, Christ was not "among us" for me either, and that all I was left with were the words, wondering, even then, if the words would ever be enough.

The next Lent when, at thirteen and confirmed, and knowing how to serve, I determined to keep what we called a good Lent. To go to church twice a week and, childlike, to try to get to the bottom of the mystery. Church was at seven. There was still plenty of time to catch the school bus after the service.

It had been an easy winter, not like the previous winters and certainly not like the Great Winter of the dog hunt. Even so, Lent was early that year and there was snow. My father was as usual away during the week on business, so I was the server at the seven o'clock celebrations of Communion, or what we, being High Church, called Mass.

One early morning I walked into the chancel in front of Will, who was carrying the veiled chalice, looked out to the nave of the church, and saw only one other person. So that morning in the cold church (they hadn't yet installed central heating) there would be only the three of us—and the mystery and the words.

In a church procession the most important person comes last, until we come to the step and I move aside and Will goes into the sanctuary to arrange the veiled chalice and open the altar book. Then I kneel on the bare wooden floor, waiting, balanced. I can kneel for thirty-five minutes without feeling faint and have learned to keep my back straight, so my weight goes to my knees.

He returns to the foot of the sanctuary and stands while I remain kneeling, still tense, but cautiously hopeful. It is about to start. He begins, "In the name of the Father," while making the sign of the cross. After we say the psalm, he turns to me, bowing, and says, "I confess to God Almighty, before the whole company of heaven, and to you . . ." Here he is to say "to you my brethren," meaning everyone in the church.

But that morning, halfway into my first Lent, he made a mistake and said "to you my brother." To me alone. And I felt a sudden warmth as if God himself had finally spoken to me; and for that moment the steady and inexorable loss of my world became bearable, even at thirteen.

FUNERALS ARE THE reason I go back now. They seem to happen particularly in the winter, as the old people die off, and I come from wherever I happen to be. Each time I return, the road west from the town —now a city—is overlaid with more memory, like the layers of features on a new style map: topography, roads, towns, villages. Each layer is added on until it is all there—everything you could possibly want to know about the countryside and your own life—laid out in one case by modern science and, in the other, memory. Of course, the church has changed again and again. That is what they wanted, my father and Will—to take the little country brick church and make it a thing of small but rare beauty. They wanted it to have a large stone altar, a pipe organ, lots of vesting rooms, the modern-medieval windows. Those windows were made in Holland, and when they arrived at the village Will and my father were so excited that Daddy installed one of them himself instead of waiting for the experts. They were proud of themselves and the beauty of the window, until two weeks later the whole thing buckled and the experts barely saved it.

Each time I enter the church I look for the galvanized pulley still nailed into the rafters high above the nave, which my father put there in 1948 for the Christmas pageant. They tried to make the pageant a Broadway show with a stage. The pulley was to pull up the curtain. But my father only got as far as running a rope through it before Will jerked him back to reality and to the fact that it was a church and not a theater —curious for one of High Church persuasion. So no more theater—obviously not necessary to salvation. But the little galvanized pulley remained as a memory for me of my father and Will, a mark of their passing, hung high above the nave—having survived the latest remodeling and expansion—to hold up the curtain that time they all got so carried away over Christmas.

Until the last time. It was gone. The shock was physical. My gut tightened. Well, I suppose I always knew it would happen, knew that one day I would walk into the church for a funeral to discover that my little symbol for them was gone, that all that was left of the old church seemed to be the nave, somehow dwarfed by the rest: the choir loft and the little pipe organ my father spent so many hours on and the clear chancel. There is one other thing left: the reredos behind the altar, carved from oak stained black, with the wheat sheaves for the bread on one side of the cross and the grapes for the wine on the other. But as for the nave, the pine pews are too small, the wood too soft with too many scratches, too primitive. The next time the pews would be gone, too. I was sure. And as if to put it into some dusty archive in my mind, I looked across and back, thinking of the people who from custom used the same pew, year after year.

And then toward the back on the Gospel side, I saw him as clear as day. It was from a time when just the two of us were there, Will standing with his hands resting on the pew in front of him, smiling and then suddenly that laugh, a horse laugh I always called it. Being a kid, I had been shocked and had rebuked him. Laughter in church! He gave an absolutely straight-faced answer: "This is God's house and I'm at home here." Then, in spite of everything, he smiled.

And at the smile the scene in my mind's eye suddenly shifted back to the Sunday morning of the moccasin, with the snake turning back on himself to miss the root as he crawled away from us, me waiting for the lecture, and Will, smiling, asking me in his serious funny way if I wanted to learn to serve at the altar—and feeling the lurch of my heart at the unexpectedness of the thing. And me thinking—now, not then—that in spite of my inclination to symbolize, that that snake was not the ancient symbol, not the creature of the garden. No, just *Agkistrodon piscivorus*, the cottonmouth, the water moccasin, crawling quickly away after interrupting our Sunday morning. Just a snake, but dangerous, and not something to step on barefoot on any day, no matter how tight his circles or great your need to know.